# HOT SEAL, AUSTRALIAN NIGHTS

## SEALS IN PARADISE

BECCA JAMESON

D1603278

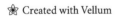

# ACKNOWLEDGMENTS

I'd like to thank my daughter and my husband for reading through this book to make sure I didn't mess up any of the events in Australia! You guys rock! My memory isn't nearly as reliable as theirs. Sigh...

Thanks to my editor, Christa, for working hard up to the last minute. And wow, my proofreader, Allison, who stayed up super late to get this done in time for me! I don't usually operate so close to a deadline, but this book got away from me. I have the most amazing team. You guys are the best.

Thanks to all the authors in the SEALs in Paradise series! You are so much fun to work with! Can't wait for the next round. SEALs in Paradise Wedding Edition: Coming 2020!

- Hot SEAL, Tijuana Nights by Cat Johnson
- Hot SEAL, Hawaiian Nights by Elle James
- Hot SEAL, Savannah Nights by Kris Michaels
- Hot SEAL, Vegas Nights by Parker Kincade

- Hot SEAL, Australian Nights by Becca Jameson
- Hot SEAL, Roman Nights by Teresa Reasor
- Hot SEAL, Alaskan Nights by Cynthia D'Alba
- Hot SEAL, New Orleans Nights by Delilah Devlin

# CHAPTER 1

Justus Kirkland was exhausted when he stepped into the hotel in Sydney. Jet lag was going to kill him one of these days. Considering how many years he'd been with the SEALs, one would think he'd have overcome his inability to orient when he landed, but it had never happened.

Nope. While most people glancing at Justus saw a large, manly man with enormous muscles, tattoos, and an obvious military haircut, inside he was exhausted, had a fierce headache, and felt nauseous from all the time-zone hopping.

The flight from LAX had been fifteen hours long. It had also been packed, so though he'd flown through the night, he had not gotten more than a few hours' sleep, and those few hours hadn't been sequential.

He checked into his room, gladly handed his suitcase over to the bellman, and then reluctantly turned toward the guest services desk. What he wanted to do was sleep. However, he'd promised his best friend and fellow SEAL, Tony, he would touch base with the man's sister first thing.

Arianna Gallo. She was expecting him. He hadn't seen

her in several years, and he wasn't looking forward to it today either. Not just because he was tired, but because he'd managed to get roped into letting her plan his itinerary.

Justus needed this vacation. He'd been on assignment in Djibouti with the SEAL team for six months. He was mentally exhausted from the stress and looking forward to ten days of leave. And here he was being forced to let his best friend's sister play tour guide when all he wanted was to be left alone to relax.

Justus hadn't thought about Arianna in years. He actually hadn't thought much about her in general. She was simply Tony's gangly little sister, younger than him by four years. When Justus and Tony graduated high school and joined the navy, Arianna had been fourteen years old.

He'd seen her briefly several times in the following years, but his mind remembered a slender young girl who'd grown tall for her age but hadn't filled out yet. She'd had wild, curly, unruly hair and giggled a lot. He hadn't crossed paths with her in the last few years because she'd been at college, and somehow his leave never coincided with her breaks.

Justus hadn't known Arianna was even in Australia until he'd mentioned his travel plans to Tony. Tony, being the overprotective Italian brother he was, implored Justus to check up on his little sister and make sure she was okay.

That might have been fine, but Tony took it a step further and had emailed Arianna to inform her Justus would be arriving. And Justus's entire vacation plans snowballed out of control from there. He'd gotten a lengthy email from Arianna hours later informing him she had basically hijacked his vacation and would ensure he had the trip of a lifetime.

Justus nearly groaned out loud as he wandered toward

the guest services desk. An attractive woman with thick, smooth hair that reached the middle of her back was standing behind the desk, her gaze locked on the computer, her hand on the mouse. If only *this* woman were the one who'd taken over his vacation.

"Excuse me," Justus began. "I'm looking for Arianna Gallo. She's supposed to meet me here this morning."

The woman lifted her gaze. For a heartbeat, she simply stared at him, and then a slow smile spread across her face as her cheeks flushed. "You're here."

He frowned at her, thinking that was the oddest thing to say. Had Arianna described him to her coworkers? *Great.*

When she circled the small podium, stepped into his space, and wrapped her arms around him, he stopped breathing. What the hell? His arms hung awkwardly at his sides while she squeezed him, her head under his chin. Two things stood out immediately—her hair smelled amazing, like vanilla and raspberry, and her ample breasts pressed against his chest.

After several moments, she leaned back a few inches, tipping her head to meet his gaze. Her eyes were dancing with laugher, and she was smiling even wider. She slid a hand around to pat his chest. "You don't recognize me."

He stared into her deep, brown eyes, absorbing the olive coloring of her skin and her high cheekbones before he blinked and opened his eyes wider. "Arianna?" *Holy shit.*

She laughed, a mid-range pitch that spread through his body and settled in his cock. The last thing he needed was to have her pressed against his growing erection. *Jesus.* So, he grabbed her waist and forced some space between their bodies.

She tipped her head to one side. "I've probably changed a bit since the last time you saw me."

3

*You think?* He swallowed. "Understatement." He released her waist with one hand and reached for her hair, running his fingers through it before he could stop himself. "What happened to the curls?"

She laughed again, all that thick hair swaying as she shoved off his chest and put a bit more distance between them. "Straighteners and products. I'm not a kid anymore."

"I see that," he murmured before he could stop himself. His gaze dipped to travel down her body. The gangly, flat-chested girl he remembered now had boobs and curves. She wore a white blouse he could see through enough to notice a white lace bra. Forcing his gaze lower, he took in her navy pencil skirt that hit above her knees. Long, olive-skinned legs. Navy pumps.

He yanked his gaze back to her hair as she turned around and stepped behind the small desk. She picked up a piece of paper and lifted her eyes. Her face was flushed, and she licked her lips. "I printed your itinerary in case you didn't."

He nodded, unable to respond. How the hell was this sexy, grown woman Tony's baby sister?

She kept speaking. "I figured you would need to sleep for a while this morning, so I didn't plan anything until this afternoon. You want to meet me at two o'clock?"

For another moment, he simply stared at her, not fully soaking in her words. Maybe fatigue was the cause, but he suspected shock had a lot more to do with it.

"You're exhausted, aren't you?" she asked, her eyes narrowing. "Did you get your room key?"

He held it up. "Yep."

"Why don't you go lie down for a while, then?" she suggested.

His feet wouldn't move. Finally, he shook himself out of the weird stupor and nodded. "Good plan. Two, you say?"

"Yes. I'll come to your room if you **want?** What number is it?"

He glanced at the number scribbled on the outside of his key sleeve. "1520."

"Got it. I'll just meet you there." She pointed across the lobby. "The elevators are right over there. I'm sure someone will bring your luggage up shortly if they haven't already."

He scanned her face again, trying to reconcile this adult woman with the girl he'd known. It had been ridiculous of him to think she would look like she had as a teenager, but he honestly hadn't conjured up any other image.

He cleared his throat. "Sounds good. I'll see you in a few hours, then." Somehow he managed to turn around and head for the elevators.

When he got to his room, his luggage had indeed beat him. He didn't need anything in it, however. He needed sleep. So, he kicked off his shoes, tugged back the white comforter on the king-sized bed, and nearly face-planted onto the cool sheets.

His mind was still reeling over the image of Arianna Gallo. A woman. An attractive one with a sexy voice and a killer body. Tony's sister. Off limits. He closed his eyes, willed her image out of his mind, and fell asleep quickly.

# CHAPTER 2

Arianna stood outside Justus's room that afternoon with her hand lifted to knock. She hesitated, lowered her hand, and took a deep breath. This was Justus Kirkland, the man she'd pined over as a teenager, thinking he was the sexiest person she'd ever seen in her life.

She'd spent countless hours fantasizing what it would be like to kiss him. What his lips would feel like against hers. His hard body pressing her against a wall. Or a door. Or a bed.

She closed her eyes and inhaled again. The muscular body she remembered from her freshman year of high school when he and Tony had left for basic training had taken her breath away on a number of occasions. She'd assumed her mind had exaggerated the visual over the years. But she'd been wrong. The man who'd approached her that morning had been even larger, buffer, and sexier.

Damn. She was in so much trouble.

When Tony had emailed her asking her to meet up with Justus and help him get the lay of the land, she'd known immediately his real motive had been to have Justus check up on her. She'd also known immediately that *her* real motive would be to spend some time with her brother's hunky friend. She doubted Tony had any idea his little sister had lusted after his best friend so many years ago, nor that she might jump at this opportunity to see if the sparks still existed. At least for her.

So far, the answer was *yes*. Not just sparks, but flames that reached higher than she'd expected. It had taken every ounce of energy she had to speak to him without stammering that morning. Meanwhile, Justus had seemed stunned and shell-shocked. Although, he'd probably simply been too tired to make conversation.

She hadn't missed the way he looked up and down her body, though. The way his gaze lingered on her chest and then her hips and then her legs. The way he swallowed as he jerked his gaze back to her face.

It had probably been a bad idea to take time off work in order to play tour guide for this man. For one thing, she'd done so without consulting him. For another thing, what had originally seemed like a harmless plan to flirt with and drool over a hot man was probably going to bite her in the ass.

Yeah, he was sex on a stick, but she'd visualized a fun diversion, not a panty-melting body slam. After only five minutes in his company, she realized she could fall for him, which was totally against her personal policy. *I do not date military men. Ever.*

Taking yet another breath, she squared her shoulders and knocked. She waited a few moments, hearing nothing from the other side of the door, and then she knocked again, harder.

There was a shuffling noise this time, and finally the door opened. A very rumpled Justus ran a hand through his hair and then rubbed his eyes. "Shit. Is it already two?"

"Yep. I'm so sorry. You were asleep." *Obviously*. She took a step back. "I woke you. If you want to go back to sleep..."

He held the door wider, shaking his head. "No. I'm going to be totally fucked up as it is. I should have set my alarm. Come in."

She ducked under his arm and made her way into the room. His suitcase stood next to the wall and the only evidence anyone had been in the room at all was the messy comforter.

She turned around when she reached the desk. Justus was wearing the same clothes as that morning, having only kicked off his shoes at some point. "I'm sorry," she repeated, cringing. She slid off her jacket and purse and set them on the desk.

"It's fine. I can't believe I slept that hard or that long. I don't think I have in months. Probably longer."

She nodded, biting her lower lip. She understood all too well. With two older brothers in the military, she knew better than most how little sleep enlisted men got.

"I don't think I thanked you properly for planning and arranging everything for me. I certainly didn't have time to do so myself."

"You're welcome. It was my pleasure. It's what I love to do. I can make a dollar stretch a very long way." *Now would be a super good moment to tell him you made duplicate plans for yourself.* Instead, she smiled at him.

Justus heaved his suitcase onto the bed. He unzipped it and flipped it open. "I'll just take a quick shower if you don't mind." He glanced at her and then narrowed his gaze. "Assuming you meant to show me around a bit this afternoon. I don't mean to interrupt any plans you have. I can manage on my own."

She shook her head. "No. Of course not. I'm all yours." She pulled out the desk chair and lowered onto it, crossing her legs. It took effort not to fidget or swing her top leg as she watched him move.

His jeans hung low on his hips, and the SEAL T-shirt he wore stretched across his chest in a way that left nothing to the imagination. She'd felt all that muscle against her cheek when she'd hugged him that morning. Power. Dominance. Confidence. She'd imagined him in many scenarios over the years, but their morning reunion had left her thinking she'd underestimated him. He was more than her daydreams had conjured.

Every muscle in his arms flexed as he grabbed a toiletry bag from his suitcase. "Do you work later today?"

She swallowed. "No." *Now. Arianna. Tell him.* She had no idea how he was going to react when he found out she'd taken time off to spend with him? Maybe she should wait. It had been too easy since he'd taken Tony's word for it that she was a great vacation planner. He'd given her a budget and then emailed her all his personal information and the necessary funds to make arrangements for him. She'd saved for nine months and had plenty of spending money to join him.

"Okay, I'll be quick." He pointed over his shoulder and then backed toward the bathroom. If his hair had been longer, it would be messy, but he had a very short military cut. The only thing scruffy about him was the two-day-old beard growth from traveling. She half hoped he would leave it. The other half of her wondered what he looked like clean-shaven these days.

Seconds after the bathroom door snicked shut, the water was on. Arianna glanced down at herself, wondering how he saw her. Earlier she'd been totally professional. She'd since changed. Now, she wore her best tight jeans she knew accentuated her ass perfectly. She also had on a thin, white sweater that hugged her chest in a way that made men's heads turn. White tennis shoes rounded out the outfit.

She'd aimed for comfortable but flirty. She had no idea if Justus had even noticed yet. He'd made very little eye contact with her. Then again, he'd been half-asleep.

Nerves attacked her, making her heart race and her palms sweat. The room smelled like Justus already, even though he'd done nothing but sleep in there for a few hours. His scent had changed since she'd been barely more than a child. The underlying scent was still all Justus, but he'd changed his deodorant or aftershave or something. She liked it.

A glance at his open suitcase made her smile. Everything was professionally packed. She shouldn't be surprised. Her brothers always came home with bags that looked like that, a result of years of ingrained military training. She wondered if Justus's need to be precise extended to every aspect of his life on vacation or not. She would soon find out.

When the door to the bathroom opened and Justus stepped back into the room in a fog of steam, she jumped in her seat. For one thing, he'd been very fast. For another thing, he wore nothing more than a towel around his hips.

*Jesus.*

His broad shoulders made her mouth water. His skin was sun-kissed and flawless. Tattoos extended down both biceps. The towel slipped lower on his hips, making her wish it would fall to the ground so she could see his fine ass.

She held her breath while he tugged a few items from his suitcase and then turned around, gracing her with a view of another tattoo between his shoulder blades. He didn't make eye contact as he returned to the bathroom, so she let her gaze roam to the front of his towel, her thoughts shifting to what lay beneath. The bathroom door shut again, and Arianna finally exhaled. She needed to get a grip or she was going to make a fool of herself before the end of one hour with this man.

Five minutes later, he returned, clean jeans, another tight T-shirt—this one navy with no logo—and bare feet. He sat on the edge of the bed and put on socks and then tennis shoes. Finally, he stood. "I think I'm half alive now. No promises." He gave her a half grin that only lifted one corner of his mouth and made her insides melt. His eyes twinkled at the same time, making her wonder if he looked at all women like that.

She pushed to standing, hoping she could avoid tripping over her own feet or falling on her face. "It's warm out this afternoon. I thought we might take the ferry up and down the harbour so you can get an overview. We'll start at Circular Quay and head toward Watsons Bay and then we can wander around for a while. There is an amazing view of the ocean from Gap Bluff. Then we can jump back on the ferry and take it to Darling Harbour. We can eat dinner someplace there."

His smile spread.

"What?" she asked self-consciously.

"Do you always talk so fast?"

She swallowed. "Maybe." *Or maybe just when I'm in a small room with a man who looks good enough to eat but is totally off limits.*

Not for the first time, she worried about the prudence of her decision to play tour guide to this man. What the hell had she been thinking? He was going to leave her tongue-tied and nervous every day. She doubted anything she'd said made sense. Something about him made her feel like the teenage girl who'd crushed on him.

Arianna lifted her jacket and shrugged into it. At least it

gave her something to do. She concentrated on zipping the front a few inches in order to avoid staring at him, and then she swung her purse over her shoulder. "You might want something with sleeves. It's nice out now, but this is winter here. It will be chilly later."

"How chilly?" he asked, lifting a brow.

"Forty-five at night."

He chuckled. "That sounds like heaven. I've been hot for six straight months with no air conditioning. While most of the guys on my team chose to vacation in summer locations, I chose winter."

"It's not much of a winter here. We're too close to the equator."

"Yeah, but temperatures between forty-five and sixty-five are my kind of weather." He opened the door to the room and swept out a hand. "After you."

They walked to the elevator in silence. An awkward silence. Arianna felt like a miniature human next to Justus. She may have graduated college and spent the last nine months working and traveling in Australia, but she knew she wasn't half as worldly as him. What would they discuss?

After they stepped into the lobby and then outside, she finally felt like she might be able to breathe. At least she knew this city and all its secrets. She could busy herself playing tour guide and ignore the way her body reacted to the proximity of her childhood crush.

She was honestly stunned by her physical reaction. She'd envisioned thinking he would be attractive, not at all hard on the eyes, but she hadn't been prepared for the way her breath had left her body the moment she hugged him. The way her breath continued to stutter out of her as they strolled toward Circular Quay. As a kid she'd lusted after him for his looks. She'd been too young to grasp this physical awareness she felt now in every inch of her body.

"Thank you for getting me oriented. It's kind of you," Justus stated as he tucked the tips of his fingers in his jeans. He walked alongside her, keeping the same pace while leaving about a foot of space between them.

She shrugged. "It's my job. It's what I'm good at. I enjoy helping people plan their stay in Australia."

"Yeah, but taking the rest of the day off is above and beyond. You didn't have to do that."

They stopped at a corner because the light was red. She turned toward him and lifted her gaze, her heart beating faster. *Now. For sure now.* "I took the entire ten days off to travel with you, Justus."

His eyes grew huge, his mouth falling open. "Seriously?"

She shrugged again. "I haven't taken any time off in a while. I thought it would be fun. This way you won't miss anything." She forced a smile, waiting for his reaction.

He licked his lips and swallowed hard. "You didn't have to do that."

"I know, but I did."

"That's a lot of time off. How can you afford that?"

"I'm here on a work-and-holiday visa. The object is to see the country while earning enough money to live off. I'm ahead of the game mostly because I enjoy my job."

His gaze was narrowed. She couldn't read his expression. Was he disappointed? She hadn't considered that possibility for some reason.

When the light turned green, they started walking again, and Justus changed the subject. "Tony says you have a degree in Hospitality and Tourism Management."

"Yep. I'm hoping to eventually manage a hotel somewhere."

"You planning to return to New York?"

"Not sure yet. Maybe. I love it there, but I've lived there my entire life. It's expensive. I might be open to other possibilities. I'll probably move back in with Mom and Pop until I find a job offer that intrigues me." The thought of moving in with her parents again after being away at college and then abroad made her cringe, but it was expected. In her large Italian family, women didn't just move out for no reason. It wasn't seemly.

"I'm sure you'll find the perfect job quickly."

"What about you? How long are you planning to stay with the SEALs?"

He shrugged. "Not sure yet. I have to be back in two weeks, but I haven't decided if I want to keep going until I retire or bail at some point and do something else. It's a grueling job that takes its toll on the mind and the body."

"Yeah. I've noticed that with my brothers and cousins." So many of her family members were in the military that she had always been exposed to the less glamorous side of things. That's why she'd sworn herself off military men from the moment she'd been old enough to be attracted to them.

Sure, they were sexy. The buff muscles, cropped haircuts, tattoos, uniforms. All of it made her swoon. But with that superficial stuff came long deployments, intermittent contact, and the constant threat of death.

Even Justus had been relegated to the look-but-don't-touch compartment in her brain when he left for the navy with her brother. He might be sexy with a smile that melted her insides, but no way was she going to permit herself to fall for a man in uniform.

She'd watched two of her aunts and several cousins and wives wring their hands together and shed innumerable tears over the years. Only one uncle had been killed in battle, but the entire family stressed all the time.

It was heartbreaking watching a woman cry herself to sleep because she didn't have any idea where her husband or boyfriend was when she needed him. Arianna had watched pregnancies, miscarriages, first birthday parties, anniversaries, and countless other milestones go by while husbands remained absent.

It was not a life she wanted for herself. No way. Not a chance in hell. Flirting with Justus for a few days was the most she could endure, and only because he'd been her first real crush almost nine years ago. If nothing else, she could burn him out of her system and hopefully stop dreaming about him as if he were some sort of god.

They reached the dock. Arianna had purchased an Opal card for Justus earlier in the week, so they didn't need to stop at the kiosk to get him a ferry ticket. She led him to the ferry, handed him his card, and they boarded.

"Let's go upstairs. It might be cold in the open air, but the view will be amazing." She jogged up the stairs to the upper deck and headed through the crowd of people to the rear.

Justus stepped up next to her. "Wow. I've seen pictures, but nothing does this justice." He smiled as she watched him scan the surroundings, remembering exactly how she felt the first time she stood in this exact spot. Next to them was an enormous cruise ship that would leave the dock that evening. Behind the ship was the Harbour Bridge. When they turned to face the other way, they could see the Sydney Opera House.

"It's truly breathtaking. My favorite place on earth so far." She leaned her butt against the railing as the ferry pulled away from the dock. "Not that I've been many places, but I suspect I'm ruined for most others."

"You are," he breathed out as he leaned against the railing next to her. Only a few inches separated them, and his fingers touched her hip when he gripped the railing at his sides. "So gorgeous. How can you stand to work all day?" he teased.

"I've gotten used to it, but I do come out here often just to stand and spin around slowly and take in the view." She pointed across from the opera house as the ferry headed that direction. "The outdoor theater is across from the opera house. I've gone to two different performances there. Both times I arrived two hours early and spent that time drinking wine and watching the sunset with the Harbour Bridge and the Opera House as my backdrop. It's breathtaking."

"I bet it is."

They rode in silence for a while, during which time Arianna stole glances at Justus, often staring at him for long seconds while he took in the scenery. At the second stop, she grabbed his arm and nodded toward the stairs. "We're getting off here."

She led him to the exit and then down the long pier where they tapped their Opal cards to pay for their trip.

# CHAPTER 3

Justus was wide awake now. The fresh air and gorgeous woman at his side perked him up quickly. He probably wouldn't be able to sleep again until about four in the morning, but it would be worth it. Thank God Arianna had woken him up when she did, or else he would have slept far too long and been even more fucked up.

He was both concerned and elated that she'd taken time off work to accompany him on this vacation. The mixed emotions were probably causing him to send her mixed signals that he couldn't avoid.

On the one hand, she was gorgeous and fun and full of information. The slender teenager who'd shot coy glances at him and giggled too much was gone. This grown-up version was stunning in every way. He wondered if she had a boyfriend, and then decided it was unlikely since she'd taken time off to spend with him.

On the other hand, she was off limits. Totally off limits. She was Tony's little sister, not some girl in a port he could fuck and walk away from. Tony had asked him to check up on her, make sure she was safe, not sleep with her. Did he have any idea Arianna had arranged to play tour guide for the week? Probably not.

And what about the rest of her large family? How much did they know about Justus's trip to Australia? Enzo and Maryanne Gallo were currently in Rome for their thirty-fifth wedding anniversary. That's also where Tony had gone on his leave. Arianna was the only member of the family who hadn't been able to join since she was in Australia for the year.

Justus closed his eyes for a few moments, recalling the numerous times he'd spent at the Gallo house in his teens. He and Tony had met their freshman year of high school. In many ways, they were polar opposites. What they had in common was their love for sports. So, they'd become fast friends.

Tony's parents had always treated Justus like he was a member of the family. He'd eaten amazing Italian dinners at their house more times than he could count. He'd hung out with Tony at their restaurant. He knew the Gallos loved him. He seriously doubted they would approve of him traveling with their oldest daughter.

There were a dozen other reasons why Justus needed to keep his eyes and hands off her. For one thing, this was the only time he would probably see her this year. If she were a stranger he hooked up with on vacation, that would be one thing. Someone with whom he had a clear understanding that he would never see them again. But he wouldn't dare start something with someone he knew. Because this vacation would come to an end, and he wouldn't risk hurting her.

Not to mention the fact that he didn't do relationships. Ever. Many of his fellow SEALs had wives or girlfriends. He watched them deal with the trials of maintaining long-distance relationships and wanted nothing to do with it.

Significant others were a distraction. Nothing but frustration that came from trying to keep the flames alive.

All of that aside, Justus was walking a dangerously thin line so far. He'd only been with Arianna for an hour and already he felt drawn to her. As they strolled past an outdoor fish restaurant headed to an unknown destination, he set a hand on the small of her back.

It took him several moments to realize how stupid that unintentional display was and remove his fingers to tuck them in his back pocket. She said nothing, but tipped her face back and smiled at him. "This is Robertson Park. We're heading toward Gap Bluff. You're going to love this view." She pointed straight ahead through the park toward a rock wall. From where they walked, he couldn't imagine what they were going to see, but he trusted her. Already. Implicitly.

Yes. His initial reaction to her proclamation that she intended to spend the entire vacation with him had been shock and hesitation, but he knew within minutes that it would be no hardship. Still, was it a good idea?

Why the hell had she given up all this time to spend with a man she'd only known as her brother's childhood friend? That had been risky. And it still made him nervous. She was going to be a trial to his sanity. Another glance in her direction told him he was going to be taking a lot of cold showers too.

The woman had a body that made his mouth dry. Perfect curves and amazing tits that drew his attention. He couldn't shake the desire to run his hands up and down her skin.

She was also full of life and energy. She nearly bounced on her feet as she led him to a set of stone stairs and then climbed them. He jogged to keep up, smiling at his good fortune, determined to enjoy staring at her fantastic ass while keeping his cock in his pants. He could do that, right?

His eyes were on her when they reached the top, so it took him a moment to catch the view out of his peripheral vision. Finally, he turned toward the sea and his breath whooshed out. "Damn," he murmured, grabbing the edge of the stone wall in front of him. They were high above a bay with nothing but ocean for as far as he could see.

"It's amazing, isn't it?" she asked as she stepped closer until her arm pressed against his. Even through the jacket and her sweater, he could feel the heat of her, and it stirred something in him he needed to get a grip on fast.

"You're looking at Watsons Bay. You should take pictures," she pointed out, lifting her face. "It's a once in a lifetime sight. Do you have your phone?"

He narrowed his brow. "I'm not much of a pictures kind of guy. Even if I took them, they would forever be stuck in the ether on my phone."

She laughed and pulled hers out of her pocket. "Fine. We'll use mine. I don't leave my pictures in the ether," she joked. "My family would have a coronary if they didn't see at least weekly updates from me on social media."

He chuckled, having no doubt she was telling the truth. With two older brothers, two younger siblings, parents who held all their children close, and countless uncles, aunts, and cousins, about a dozen people would lose their shit in a heartbeat if she didn't stay in constant contact, especially traveling outside of the country.

Tony had always been especially protective of everyone in his family as the eldest son. But Arianna was the oldest daughter. Tony had started shooting glares at any boy who looked her way from a young age. Justus had found his friend's overprotectiveness hilarious back then. Now, he shuddered, wondering what his friend might think of not just boys, but men, ogling his little sister, who was definitely not so little anymore.

As an only child, Justus had never been able to relate to the tightness of the Gallo family. Justus's own parents had both worked full-time. His mother as a teacher; his father as an electrician. In contrast to Tony's house, Justus's home was quiet and boring.

Arianna shook him back to the present when she handed him her phone. He spun around, wrapping one arm around her shoulders as she started to step away. "Get in it with me. A selfie." He lifted the phone and snapped the photo. How many of these would he take in the next ten days?

She leaned over his shot and nodded. "Better than anything I ever take. Your arms are longer, and you can reach higher."

He handed it back to her and then reached a finger up to tuck a lock of hair behind her ear without thinking.

Her breath caught, and she tipped her cheek toward his palm.

He jerked his hand back and turned to face the water again. *Shit.* So much trouble.

"You're not kidding. This is truly one of the most beautiful places I've ever been in my life," he stated as they rode the ferry into Darling Harbour. Arianna took about a dozen pictures of them as they glided through the water.

She leaned into him again, lifting a finger. "That's Pyrmont Bridge. We'll walk across it and eat dinner on the other side of the harbour."

As they exited the ferry, Justus took one of hundreds of deep breaths. He liked this woman. A lot. Too much. Why did the first woman to tempt him in years have to be Arianna Gallo?

After another selfie, she grabbed his hand innocently and tugged him toward the bridge.

He smiled at the back of her, unable to stop himself. After months of stressful serious work in Djibouti ending with an intense mission in Yemen, he couldn't remember the last time he'd smiled so often, or even at all. Yes, he'd enjoyed a fun night with the rest of his team at McP's in Coronado Island before traveling to Australia, but before that, he'd gone months without a break of any kind. His team had used that night to unwind a bit as a unit, reacclimate themselves with regular society before splitting up and going their separate ways.

Hell, even that night could hardly count as a break considering he'd spent it in the company of his team. Not a woman. And certainly no one nearly as appealing as Arianna.

Maybe the real reason he was so attracted to Arianna was because he hadn't been with a woman for so long. Maybe it had nothing to do with her personally.

*Right. Keep telling yourself that.*

She released his hand to stop in the middle of the pedestrian bridge and lean against the green railing. Her face flushed, and he realized he was staring at her instead of the view.

He jerked his gaze toward the harbour and rested a hip on the railing next to her. If this were a date, it would rank as the best one he'd ever been on. She was so easy to be with. After taking in the view of various restaurants, shopping, and tourist attractions, he resumed looking at her profile.

"When did you change your hair?" he asked without thinking. He even lifted a hand to stroke down the length of it before he could stop himself. He found himself making every possible internal excuse to touch her.

She shrugged. "I don't know. Probably senior year of high school or whenever I realized I was never going to get a date to any school dance with those out-of-control curls sticking out in every direction."

He shifted his gaze from the smooth, grown-up version of her thick, dark hair to her face again as he let the soft lock fall through his fingers. He cleared his throat, knowing he needed to address the elephant nearly shoving them off the side of the bridge. "This wasn't supposed to happen."

"What wasn't supposed to happen?" she whispered.

"You. Me. The chemistry between us."

She tucked her lips under her teeth.

"You're attractive and fun and sweet and so many other things. My thoughts around you are not appropriate."

She released her lips. "I could say the same about you."

He feared she would say that. A mutual attraction was even worse. "There are nine hundred reasons why I shouldn't touch you."

She leaned in closer and flattened a hand on his chest, her hair blowing in the breeze while they stood in the center of this bridge in one of the most romantic places on earth. "You've already touched me."

He smirked, setting his hand on top of hers and pressing her fingers into his pecs. Her skin was so soft. When he glanced down at their connection, it took his breath away. Her fingers darker than his, smaller, perfectly manicured pink nails, dainty. He wanted to lift those fingers to his lips and kiss the tip of every one.

Instead, he shifted his gaze back to meet hers. "We can't get involved. Tony asked me to check up on you. I'm certain that was all he intended."

She rolled her eyes. "Spare me a lecture about overprotective brothers. Tony isn't here. I'm a grown adult. What I do with my time is none of his business."

"Yeah, well. *I* would know, and there's no way in hell I could face him when I return to base if I slept with his sister."

She shrugged. "So, we won't *sleep*."

He groaned. "Arianna…"

"Why does it have to be such a big deal? How about if we just go with the flow and see what happens?"

"Because you're not some woman I just met who's interested in a fling."

She shrugged. "Why the hell not?"

He narrowed his eyes. "Because I would never do that to you, even if Tony weren't your brother. You're not that kind of woman. I'm not a relationship guy. I have nothing to offer anyone. My entire focus for all but four weeks out of every year is on saving lives and staying alive myself. I've never wanted to be involved long-term with a woman. It's a choice I made years ago. I see what it does to the rest of my team when they have to worry about someone other than themselves. It can put lives in danger."

He lowered his voice, taking a deep breath. "I'm married to my job. I don't have time for a woman."

"Whoa." She leaned back, tugging her hand free of his tight grip. "Who said anything about a relationship? If that's what you're worried about, you can ease your mind on that right now. I don't date military men. Ever. For the same reasons you just listed. While you've watched what it does to your team, I've spent my life watching what it does to my relatives and friends, the ones left behind. The ones who worry and cry and stress over men they rarely see and have no idea where they're even located. I've watched women give birth alone and raise kids alone and devote themselves to a very stressful life of single parenthood." She shook her head rapidly. "I never want that, so don't worry about me looking for anything long-term."

*Jesus.* Her words shocked him. They also unnerved him. He couldn't picture her having a fling and then walking away. He couldn't even picture himself doing so, not with Arianna. Not with Tony's sister.

"The point is we agree on this issue, so it's not an issue."

He smirked again. "Except it is, because Tony is still your brother."

"So don't tell him. He's not my keeper, Justus. He doesn't get to decide who I date or even who I sleep with. I'm sure he still thinks I'm some virginal girl who hasn't been kissed." She laughed.

Justus winced. *He* would also like to think that were true, even if it was unrealistic.

She groaned. "Come on, Justus. I'm twenty-three years old. You don't really think I'm a virgin, do you?"

Now he cringed. "Can we perhaps not talk about your sex life with other men?" He gripped the railing with his left hand, trying to shake away images of Arianna in bed with another man. Another man who wasn't himself.

She laughed again. "Sure. If it makes you feel better."

"It does." He rubbed his forehead, staring at her. Dammit. What a mess. The only reason he'd brought this subject up was because he needed to put his foot down and ensure she didn't have any ideas. Apparently, she *did* have ideas and his plan had just backfired on him.

If Tony were here, he would have a coronary. Wouldn't he? Justus thought back on all the times Tony had brought up Arianna over the years. The man had grumbled about her date to senior prom, ranting about knowing the guy's older brother and hoping Arianna's date wasn't as handsy as he remembered his brother was with the girls.

When Arianna had gone to college, Justus had overheard Tony lecturing her about college boys and their one-track minds over Skype. At the time, Justus had chuckled to himself. Now, standing here in this gorgeous setting with a fully grown-up Arianna, seeing her as a woman—someone he would definitely hit on if she were anyone else—Justus could picture Tony punching him in the face for the thoughts running through his mind.

# CHAPTER 4

Holy shit. Arianna could not wrap her mind around this latest development. Before today, Justus had never looked at her for more than a passing glance. Of course that had been years ago, but she'd had visions of a man who would see her as nothing more than a young girl.

Yes, she had hoped. Plotted. Planned this trip for him. She hadn't truly expected him to be interested in her, though. She'd simply thought it would be fun to spend time with him no matter how much of himself he shared.

To say she was shocked by today's events was an understatement.

Not once since he'd arrived had he looked at her the way he had when she was young. Every time she caught him staring at her, his gaze was smoldering in a way that made her breasts swell and her sex clench. Her panties had been wet since early that morning.

There was an intensity in his eyes that told her he was usually a serious man, which shouldn't surprise her considering how dangerous his job was and how much responsibility he shouldered. Tony often had the same look.

It was a look that came from men who'd seen too much and kept secrets buried so deep they would never talk of them. It was a look she'd seen on many of her relatives and others who'd spent any time overseas fighting for their country.

But it was more than that. He seemed to peer into her deeper than anyone ever had as if he could somehow manage to know her better if he stared hard enough.

She shivered under the scrutiny, getting the feeling she was not wrong. He could read her well.

As they stood on that bridge, something changed between them. An unspoken agreement of sorts. Maybe it wouldn't be today, but she knew they were going to wind up in bed together. She also knew it was going to be amazing and confusing and earth-shattering. In ten days, he would leave, and she would be left alone.

But it would be worth it. This brief vacation with Justus Kirkland was all she would ever get. It would have to last a lifetime, so she intended to make every second count.

For now, she needed to change the subject fast to avoid him turning her down before anything even started between them. She needed more time to convince him to let go of his obvious concerns and enjoy a fling with her.

"Hungry?" she asked, breaking the weird spell.

He nodded. "I could eat, though my body is totally confused from jet lag."

She reached for his arm and boldly slid her palm down his muscles until she reached his hand. Threading their fingers together, she took a step back. "Let's go eat."

They wandered through the shopping district on the other side of the harbour, not saying anything. He hadn't balked at her holding his hand, and in fact he switched their grip and kept her close to his side.

Her heart beat faster as they meandered through the crowd of people gathering to shop and dine after work. His warmth spread up her arm and into her body.

Yeah, they had crossed a line, one they seemed to have mutually agreed upon without specifically stating as much. It was enough that they both had aired their concerns about the future and made it clear neither of them was interested in anything beyond this trip.

It was possible he still had reservations, but he was just going to have to get over himself. She didn't care if he chose to lie about their shared vacation or be truthful. She would abide by whatever he decided.

Justus suddenly lifted his gaze. "Hey look, a Hard Rock Café. How about here?"

She smiled. "Ten thousand restaurants in Sydney, and you want to eat at Hard Rock?"

He shrugged. "It's iconic. Come on." He tugged on her arm and entered the chain restaurant. Five minutes later they were seated near a window that overlooked the harbour, fortunate enough to have scored a booth with a view.

"Gotta warn you," he stated as soon as the waiter handed them menus and left them to ponder the selections, "I plan to drink my way across this country. Beer, I mean. I intend to try every single local brew I can get my hands on."

She smiled, knowing she was going to shock him. "I can do that. I enjoy beer. In fact, I've already been here nine months. I know my way around the local breweries."

He stared at her again for a long time, his lips lifted in a smile. And then he shook his head and resumed perusing the menu. "I'm in so much trouble," he mumbled.

When the waiter came, Justus ordered a Redback Original from the Matilda Bay Brewing Company. She nodded at the waiter, indicating she would have the same thing.

As soon as they were alone again, Justus set his elbows on the table and leaned forward. "My internal clock is messed up. I don't know if it's morning, noon, or night."

"Yeah, it takes a few days to acclimate. I found it's much worse coming to a time zone eighteen hours ahead than any other place I've ever been. I'm not looking forward to the return either. I've heard it can take two weeks to recover, especially when it comes to meals and sleeping."

"I hope that doesn't happen. I won't have that option. I'll be back on base expected to have my head screwed on straight the next day."

"Good luck with that," she teased.

"I think I'm the only member of the team who went to the other side of the world for leave."

She set her chin on her palm and leaned toward him. She loved the timbre of his voice and encouraged him to continue talking. "Where did everyone else go?"

"Oh, God. All over. Tony's in Rome, of course, for your parents' anniversary party."

"Yep."

"Jace went to Hawaii. Rio went to Savannah. T-Bone went to New Orleans. Levi went to Alaska. And Aidan went to Vegas. Zach was planning to stick around home, but I heard he ended up heading for Tijuana." He gifted her with one of his dazzling smiles that made her shiver.

"Wow. You guys worked hard to make sure you didn't run into each other," she joked.

He laughed, his eyes crinkling at the corners. "It seems that way. I tried to talk Rocket into coming with me to Australia, but he declined."

"Which one's Rocket?"

"Aidan. Sorry. He decided he'd rather hit the open road on his motorcycle." Justus's face lit up when he spoke of his SEAL team. They were like brothers.

Damn, he was good looking. Everything about him, from his height to his muscular body to his intense face. She'd noticed women giving him a double take everywhere they went. Some men too.

Could she be lucky enough to claim him for the next ten days? To wrap her arm around his everywhere they went in a way that told everyone else to back off?

She stared at his lips, wondering what it would feel like to kiss him and when he might take that step. Or perhaps she could boldly do so herself. Would he be the sort of man who kissed her openly in public?

A shiver raced down her spine as she pondered the idea.

"What are you thinking?" he asked, his voice gravelly. He reached across the table and grasped one of her hands.

She hesitated, but why bother beating around the bush? If they were going to do this thing, why waste several days pretending otherwise? "I was wondering what your lips will feel like against mine. If your kisses might be rough and demanding or sweet and soft. If you're a private man or someone who doesn't mind a little PDA."

She watched him swallow, his Adam's apple bobbing as he did so. The intensity she'd grown to expect from him increased, his deep green eyes burrowing into her. His fingers gripped hers harder.

She clenched her thighs together, moisture pooling between her legs. She wished the world would disappear so that she could fuck him on this very table, to hell with propriety.

The waiter returned and set their beers down in front of them.

Without shifting his gaze from her, he ordered nachos for them to share.

Finally, he spoke to her again. "Are you always this forward?"

She shook her head, slightly embarrassed now. "No. Never. It's you. I've dreamed about you since high school. You were my first crush. And now you're here. In the flesh. Sexier than I even remembered. And the way you look at me..." Her voice trailed off. What else was there to say? He emboldened her because she could see he was a willing participant in her daydreams.

"You're playing with fire," he informed her, still pinning her to the bench seat with his gaze.

"I don't care."

"This can't go beyond this trip," he reminded her.

"I don't want it to."

The waiter showed up with their nachos, and Justus released her hand to make room on the table. He leaned back, still looking at her, his gaze making her melt. "Both," he finally said.

"Both what?" she asked, confused.

"My kisses will be both rough and demanding and soft and sweet. Depends on my mood."

She swallowed, unable to breathe.

He sat up straighter and then leaned closer. "And I'll be kissing you whenever I feel like it, without concern for who might be watching."

*Holy shit.* She might be in over her head, but she didn't care.

They slowly ate the nachos, not ordering anything else. It wasn't necessary. The plate of food was monstrous, and besides, Arianna could barely chew and swallow. All she could think about was when he might kiss her. There was no longer any need to be bold about it. She'd put the ball in his court. Now she would let him decide.

When they were finished eating, he helped her into her jacket and set a hand on the small of her back as they left the restaurant. She nearly floated as they retraced their steps and boarded the ferry. It was dark and chilly.

He led her back to the top again and took a spot where they would see the view in every direction.

She was shivering, both from cold and nerves and anticipation as she gripped the railing and looked out over the water. He set a hand on either side of hers and pressed into her back. "Cold?"

"A little." She glanced at his bare arms. "Why aren't you?"

He set his chin on her shoulder. "I told you I'm gonna need the entire trip just to cool down. I've spent months at Camp Lemonnier on the Horn of Africa. It's hotter than hell there."

She sighed and leaned against him. He reminded her that he lived in a totally different world most of the year, a world she would never understand, even if she tried. She needed to harden her heart if she was going to live through this trip, or more importantly the weeks that followed.

Because that was all she would ever get from him. Ten days. A lot could happen in ten days. A lot had happened in the last ten hours.

When they were back at Circular Quay and on the pier, he took her hand again. "Where do you live?"

She grinned at him. "In a hostel."

He flinched. "Seriously?"

"Yep. It's cheap and easy. I don't have to worry about a lease. I can move any time I want." She slid her hand up to wrap it around his arm. It was amazing how warm his skin was in the cold temperature of evening.

He frowned at her. "Is it safe?"

She smiled indulgently. "Yes. It's safe. Nothing has happened to me or my belongings in nine months. I'm good."

"Do you have your own room?"

"Nope."

His eyebrows lifted. "You share a room with strangers?"

"Yep. That's how a hostel works. I'm in a room with seven other people right now. Bunk beds. Bathroom down the hall. I don't spend much time there, so I don't care."

They continued walking. Finally, he spoke again. "Take me there."

She sighed. She would have preferred to go back to the hotel with him, although she was concerned with the looks she might get from her coworkers if she slept in one of the guest's rooms. That wasn't exactly permitted. Though her situation was different. He wasn't a stranger she met on the street. She could tell her boss anything she wanted about Justus, even that he was her boyfriend visiting from the States.

Shifting her mind from thoughts of sex with Justus, she led him begrudgingly to her hostel. When they arrived, she stopped. "This is it. You want to see the inside? We'll have to be quiet. The room is always dark because you never know who might be sleeping at any given time."

"Nah. That's okay." He shuddered. "I've been in plenty of hostels before. I don't need to see it. I know what it looks like." He squared her so that she faced him, his hands on her shoulders. "Pack your stuff and check out tomorrow. You can stay with me while I'm here. I don't want to be sneaking around your shared bunk bed trying to make out with you when I bring you back every night."

Her face heated at his words. "Okay." They were really going to do this thing. Shack up in his hotel room. She was both nervous and elated.

She was also disappointed because the next thing he did was kiss her forehead. "I'm going to go." He backed up a step.

"Now?" She crossed her arms at his loss, hugging herself.

He gave her a half grin. "Yes, Imp. Now. I need more sleep. You do too. Think hard about whether or not you really want to do this. You can back out. I won't hold it against you."

She shook her head. "I'm not backing out. Not a chance. But you can if you want." God, she prayed he didn't want.

He smirked. "Never." He took another step back. "Sleep on it, anyway. Humor me."

She nodded. "Okay."

He pointed at the door. "Go inside so I'll know you're safe."

She shook her head as she backed toward the door, still watching him. "I've been coming and going from hostels for nine months on my own. I'm pretty good at it."

"Yeah, well, not on my watch. I would never leave a woman standing in the street." He lifted his brows, nodding his head toward the door.

She reached behind her to open it. And then she was inside, their connection only broken when she shut the door. For a moment she stood in the entryway unable to move. Her body was on fire, needing something it was not going to get tonight.

She moaned as she finally dragged herself up the stairs to her shared room on the second floor. She couldn't even masturbate in this building. No way in hell could she do so quietly enough to avoid detection from her bunk bed, and the bathrooms **were** communal with stalls for showers that had nothing but curtains between them.

There was nothing she could do but wait and see what tomorrow would bring. It seemed unlikely she would sleep well. If she did fall asleep, she wondered if she would dream of Justus in the same manner she had for years.

Only one way to find out. And she suspected she would need the sleep because she had no intention of wasting a single second of her time with him in the next nine days. Sleep was not going to be high on her agenda.

## CHAPTER 5

Justus stood at the window of his hotel room in the dark for over an hour, staring at the amazing view of the Harbour Bridge and the city lights.

His dick had been hard the entire day, and it was not happy with him now. He could take himself in hand, but for some reason he found he wanted to wait. For her. For the next orgasm to belong to Arianna.

Was she currently masturbating without him? Maybe he should have told her not to, but that would have been incredibly forward. For as many things as they'd said to each other in the last several hours, he didn't think they'd reached a place in their relationship where he could order her not to touch herself.

It had been there, on the tip of his tongue while he watched her squirm, knowing she'd been disappointed that he ended the night without even kissing her. He hadn't been kidding, though. He wanted her to take the night to think about what they were planning on doing.

It wasn't a light decision. It was important. It could only be ten days. There was a good chance it would never happen again. At the very least, they both needed to go into it assuming it couldn't happen again.

He pictured her in her room on that narrow bed, a room filled with people in various stages of sleep. There was little chance she would risk touching herself in that environment, unless she was the sort of person who was incredibly quiet when she came.

He hoped that wasn't true because he intended to make her scream. Over and over again. The first time she came at his hand or from his mouth or with his cock inside her, he would know if she was a screamer or not.

*Lord.*

He ran a hand over his head. He wasn't tired. Not even close. It was day for him. Plus, he'd slept all afternoon.

He took a deep breath and let it out slowly. This was so complicated. More so for him than her. They hadn't discussed if they planned to tell her brother. That was a giant complication. He wasn't at all sure he could look Tony in the eye and lie to him for the rest of his life, but maybe his friend would never ask.

What about Arianna? Who would she tell? Would she tell her sister, Donata? He knew Donata was a few years younger, but he had no idea how close the two of them were. If Arianna told anyone at all, word would get around. It probably wasn't fair to even suggest she keep the secret. Then again, it wasn't entirely his decision.

He groaned as he closed his eyes and rested his forehead on the cool glass, shutting out the view as he retreated into his mind. At no point in the last few days had he considered this possibility.

This entire idea was wrong on so many levels it was hard to categorize them. He sensed future problems that were unimaginable at the moment. What he should do would be to face her in the morning, tell her he'd changed his mind, and leave Sydney immediately to travel to other parts of Australia. Out of sight, out of mind.

It would eliminate dealing with the stress of making poor decisions that might leave her hurt in the end. Sure, she *said* she had no interest in a relationship. She *said* she had no interest in ever dating a military man. She *said* she wanted nothing more than a fling. But could she do it?

There was a difference between them. Her lust stemmed from years of daydreaming about him. He had rarely considered her at all in those years. It put a weight on his shoulders. For one thing, he wasn't sure he could live up to her expectations. For another thing, he was concerned about how she was going to feel after he left.

Would she regret this as soon as he was gone? Would she try to contact him or pressure him into something he wasn't willing or able to give her?

Keeping this trip from her family was also an impossibility. Eyebrows would raise. They were close. It was possible the two of them could travel without much contact from Tony or the rest of her family for a while since all of them were in Rome, but no way could Justus look them in the eyes the next time he saw them and lie about whatever happened with Arianna during this vacation.

Finally, he shoved off the window. He needed to at least attempt to sleep because tomorrow would come soon enough and then he would be able to look her in the eye once again and judge where she was mentally in the light of a new day.

Maybe all his worrying would be for naught. Maybe she would show up nervously fidgeting and unable to meet his gaze, giving him his answer.

He wasn't at all sure which way he wanted this to go. Either way was dangerous. Sleeping with his best friend's sister was a bad idea. Not sleeping with her might not be an option. He was already in too deep to stop this train.

~

A noise yanked Justus out of a deep sleep. A banging sound.

Knocking.

He jerked to sitting and glanced at the clock. Light streamed into the room because he hadn't shut the curtains. Shit. He'd done it again.

He dragged himself off the bed and padded to the door, knowing he was going to owe Arianna a profuse apology for once again sleeping through her arrival.

When he opened the door, he found her standing there chewing on her bottom lip. She had two suitcases with her, one gigantic, one a carry-on. She wore another pair of jeans, this pair intentionally ripped at the knees. She had on a long-sleeved black T-shirt that hugged her breasts.

Her hair was pulled back in a ponytail at the base of her neck. She looked so young. And so fucking sexy.

She dropped her lip to comment. "I woke you again."

He reached into the hallway, grabbed the larger of her two suitcases, and hauled it inside, holding the door open for her to follow him. "I'm an ass. Sorry. I should have set an alarm. Once again, I misjudged my ability to wake up on my own."

The door shut behind her as he dragged her larger bag across the room. When he turned, he found her standing there, nervously wringing her hands. "The first few days are hard. Did you have trouble sleeping?"

He returned to the bed and sat on the edge, glad he'd at least put on loose, flannel sleep pants before he went to bed. The truth was he didn't think he'd slept more than a few hours, but he wouldn't tell her that. "I slept. I just didn't wake up."

She inched forward while he tried to judge her expression. He wanted to reach out and tug her the rest of the way toward him, situate her between his knees, stare more fully into her eyes. But he didn't dare.

She needed to have the freedom to make the first move between them today. It was huge that she'd obviously checked out of her hostel and shown up at his door. That didn't mean she couldn't still back out. She could back out at any time. He intended to make that perfectly clear.

She swallowed, glancing around his room. Nervous. "Oh, don't worry about my luggage. I'm leaving that larger one at the hotel while we're traveling."

He nodded and then ran a hand through his hair. "I swear I'm not usually this undependable. I'm a SEAL, for fuck's sake. I never oversleep. In fact, I sleep with one eye open."

She smiled at him. "You get a pass when you travel this far. It's hard."

He couldn't stand the distance another second, so he reached out a hand. "Come here."

Arianna closed the space between them, and as soon as he could reach her, he set his hand on her hip and hauled her closer. He lifted his face to meet her gaze. "I'm sorry. I swear I won't oversleep again."

She frowned at him. "It's no big deal. We have plenty of time." She shot him a shy smile. "Besides, it will be hard for you to oversleep if I'm in the same room," she teased. "Unless I let you. I might enjoy watching you sleep."

He chuckled. "That's not going to happen."

She lifted a brow. "Because you don't intend to sleep for ten days?"

"Not soundly enough for you to stare at me."

"Hmm. We'll see." Her body relaxed against his touch.

"Where are we going today?" he asked, curling his fingers into her waist a bit more. She smelled so good. He wanted to kiss her neck and inhale her scent.

"My plan is to go back to Darling Harbour to the Wild Life Sydney Zoo and then the aquarium next door. The zoo is small, but it's perfect because it only has animals you wouldn't see in the US. Koalas, kangaroos, Tasmanian devils, wallabies, cassowaries…"

"Can't wait." He smiled at her. "I'll take a quick shower."

"Take your time. No rush." She lifted a hand and caressed his neck. "I'll stand by the window and enjoy the view. It's spectacular from here."

He set his hand on top of hers and held her gaze. What he wanted to do was grab her waist with both hands, flip her onto her back on his bed, and hover over her body. He wanted to nuzzle her neck and then kiss her senseless and then strip off her clothes and then taste every inch of her skin.

He would do none of those things this morning, but he hoped he would make enough strides to do them tonight. If he let himself succumb to her allure this early in the day, they'd never make it out the door. Because he figured it would take him a number of hours to get her out of his system the first time.

Did she feel the same chemistry? He thought so. "Okay then." He stood, inched around her, and headed for the bathroom. For the second day in a row, he was going to get naked with nothing but a wall between them.

For the second day in a row, his cock was going to stiffen in his hand as he thought about her on the other side of that wall. Today was going to be different, however. Today he would claim her. Not this morning. But today. And every morning for the rest of this trip he intended to wake up with her by his side and make love to her before they ever left the bed.

*Make love? Jesus.* He stared at himself in the bathroom mirror while the water heated. Since when did he ponder the idea of "making love" instead of "having sex" or "fucking"?

*Since you stepped into Arianna's world.*

Ignoring his raging hard-on, he brushed his teeth, rushed through his shower, dried off in the steamy room, and once again emerged without anything to change into.

Arianna was leaning against the window where she'd said he would find her, but she wasn't facing the view. She was facing him, her fingers at her sides, gripping the sill. Her gaze roamed up and down his body more leisurely than yesterday.

Her cheeks were flushed and her eyes were wide.

"You okay?" he asked as he reached into his open suitcase on the luggage rack.

"Yep. Just holding onto the window sill to keep from tugging that towel off your hips. Do you deliberately tempt me by leaving your clothes in here?" she joked.

He chuckled. "No. I just wasn't thinking. I'm not used to having someone else in my room, especially not a woman. Or more precisely, especially not someone who hasn't already seen me naked."

She flinched, and he felt like an ass once again for stating it quite that way. It hadn't been necessary to point out he'd shared hotel rooms with lovers before. He certainly wouldn't want to visualize her in a similar situation. "Sorry. I didn't mean to sound like a prick."

She tipped her head to one side. "I considered taking off all my clothes and waiting for you on the bed."

He froze, his hand gripping a pair of boxer briefs tightly as if they might break if he dropped them. A groan escaped his lips. "You're going to be the death of me, aren't you?"

"Probably. After all, I'm younger. I'm more acclimated to the time zone. I have the stamina of a twenty-three-year-old."

He dropped the briefs and took three long strides to reach her. When he did, he stepped into her space, set his hands against the window pane on both sides of her head, and met her gaze with inches between them. "I have the stamina of a Navy SEAL, so don't underestimate me."

She smiled, her cheeks bright red. "Counting on it."

The sexual banter between them was intoxicating. He lowered his gaze to her lips. "If I kiss you right now, we won't be seeing any koalas today."

She licked her lips and whispered, "So you're saying you also lack willpower?"

He smirked. "I don't think you'll find me lacking anything, Arianna."

Her breath hitched as he leaned closer, her gaze traveling down toward his waist. A hair's breadth separated his cock from her belly. He wanted to press it against her so badly, but instead, he conjured up some of that willpower she'd accused him of lacking and shoved off the window.

He strode across the room, grabbed his clothes, and returned to the bathroom. His hands were shaking as he dressed. It was difficult to convince his dick to stand down and accept that it would be a full day before it got relief. But he managed.

When he returned to the bedroom, she was in the exact same spot, her mouth still hanging open. He closed the distance once again. This time, he cupped her face with both hands. "*Now* I'm going to kiss you."

"What's different about now?" she whispered, her gaze locking on his lips.

"Now I'm not wearing a precarious towel," he murmured as he lowered his face, giving her plenty of time to back out.

She lifted her hands and set them on his waist, tugging him toward her as if she had the strength to move him in any direction.

He let her, though. In fact, he pressed his body against hers as he took her lips. A tentative kiss. Gentle, easing into it. Giving her time.

But she leaned her head toward him, deepening the kiss on her own.

He spread his fingers along the back of her neck and angled her head to one side as his went the other way. God, she was amazing. He stroked his tongue along the seam of her lips, asking for entrance.

She consented, her mouth parting and her tongue reaching out to duel with his. She tasted of minty toothpaste and Arianna. Intoxicating. Delicious. Addicting. He knew in an instant he was doomed. Why couldn't she have been less attractive, less funny, less alluring? Less anything that would keep him from getting into trouble.

He deepened the kiss, consuming her, finding it difficult to stop. Not wanting to stop. Ever. He could stand here for hours locked against her. He didn't care if he never saw one single part of Australia.

Maybe they could order room service for the next nine days and never leave the room. If he got her naked, he knew he would never want her to put on clothes again.

Shaking some sanity back into his head, he finally broke off the kiss with a lick across her lips. He set his forehead against hers, fighting for oxygen. His eyes were glazed, leaving her unfocused, but he could see enough to know she was flushed. Her lips were swollen.

"Well, that answers that question," he stated when he could form words.

"Was there a question?" She smiled that beautiful smile at him.

"Not anymore." They had so much chemistry the room was going to combust.

"Agreed." Her hands slid from his waist around to his ass, which she gripped. "Shame you got dressed first."

"It was the only way I would be able to keep my dick in my pants until after we see the koalas."

She groaned. "On that note, if you want to get your picture taken next to one, we need to leave soon. I made a reservation for that part."

He lifted a brow. "You think of everything."

"I tried. I wanted you to have a great experience here. I know it's once-in-a-lifetime."

He smiled at her. "I appreciate all the work you put into it. It's going to be amazing."

She shrugged. "I love planning people's itineraries. There's nothing better than seeing the faces of vacationers when they return from a day trip I arranged. Makes my heart soar."

Yep. Arianna was vibrant and kind and wonderful in so many ways. He just hoped he could hold on to his heart during this visit.

Finally, he righted himself and stepped back. "We should go."

"We should." She didn't move an inch, though. "Give me a second to catch my breath and convince my legs to move."

He stared at her as he backed away. When the backs of his knees hit the bed, he turned and grabbed his shoes. The few moments it took him to put them on and tie them helped him pull himself together. Somewhat. Her scent permeated the room. Her shampoo or something. He had no idea what, but he knew he needed to get them out in the hall as soon as possible.

When he stood, he found she had approached. She was breathing deeply. Her pupils were dilated. Her ponytail had come loose, several strands curling around her pink cheeks. So fucking sexy.

He reached for the band containing the rest of her hair and tugged it free. After dropping it on the bed, he ran his fingers through the loose strands, spreading her hair out.

Her face was a deeper shade of red, her eyes wide.

"I like it down," he explained.

"Okay," she whispered.

He shot her a brief grin and then headed for the door. "Ready? Koalas are waiting."

# CHAPTER 6

Arianna had no idea how she was going to survive a trip to the zoo in her current state. She'd never been so aroused in her life. Her breasts were heavy and needy. She'd willed him to cup them in his palms for most of the second half of the kiss.

Her sex was wet and hot and sensitive. The only thing that made everything a little bit better was knowing his cock was also hard. She'd felt it against her belly, and she'd seen the evidence when he stepped away.

If she looked now, would he still have a bulge? She felt lucky that she could see such physical evidence. He could not. Would he be wondering if she was wet?

She could have easily come if he'd pressed his hand between her legs. Even through her jeans. Perhaps that should embarrass her, but it didn't. The thought was titillating. She'd never had this level of chemistry with anyone before. It was a new world.

She'd had sex. She'd had a few boyfriends. Nothing compared to this intensity, though. This need. This drive.

She was so totally consumed with him that she paid

attention to nothing as they descended in the elevator and then stepped into the lobby.

Justus threaded his fingers with hers and kept her close to his side as they made their way through several guests, heading for the front door. As they headed for the ferry, she pointed out the attractions. She was still talking when they arrived at the pier in Darling Harbour, stopping only when she noticed he was smiling at her indulgently. She'd been rambling on for a long time without pausing.

"You make an excellent tour guide. I should be worried."

"Why?" she asked as they stepped from the ferry.

He held her hand again. So far she didn't think he'd ever stopped touching her since they left his hotel room. Some part of him was always in contact. She liked it. "You might switch your job to tour guide after I leave, and then I'll wonder if you're retracing these steps with another man."

She sucked in a breath. "I don't think you need to worry about that." There wasn't a chance in hell another man was going to fill Justus's shoes. Perhaps not ever. She hadn't even slept with him and already she was worried about her heart. She needed to get a grip on her emotional attachment before she got hurt. This was a fling. Nothing else. Two people mutually attracted to each other who'd agreed to go on vacation together. Oh and fuck. That too.

They entered the zoo and began to wind their way around the featured animals. It was exactly the sort of place that attracted tourists. It had several floors and all of the animals were native to Australia. Animals people in the US would rarely be exposed to, if at all.

When they reached the top floor, Arianna exchanged their tickets for wristbands and they got in line to step up close to the koalas and get their picture taken.

Justus stood at her back, his arms around her body, clasped in front of her. He whispered in her ear, "They don't let you touch the koalas?"

"Nope. It's not legal in New South Wales. When we get to Queensland, you can hold one, though, and get a better picture."

"Cool. Looking forward to it."

"I haven't been there yet, but I've heard about it. I've been meaning to go for months."

"Good. We'll experience it together."

She smiled up at him. "We will."

"When are we going?"

"Did you not even glance at your itinerary?"

"Nope. I trust you."

"You gave me your credit card number and all your personal information last week and you never once noticed what I bought you?"

"Nope."

She laughed. "Well, we're going to Cairns the day after tomorrow. We're spending four days there."

"Can't wait." He leaned closer and kissed her again. She'd lost track of how many times he'd brushed his lips against hers since they'd left the hotel, but he hadn't been kidding when he promised he would kiss her wherever and whenever he wanted. He also hadn't been kidding when he promised her he would be both soft and sweet and rough and demanding. He'd been both that morning before they left his room. And she'd melted when he switched from one to the other.

She was so aroused it was hard to care about the koalas. Mostly, she just wanted the clock to move faster so that she could get back to the room with him and finish what they'd started. She was hardly paying attention when it was suddenly their turn to get pictures with the koala.

They stood next to a eucalyptus tree and smiled for the camera next to a sleeping koala hanging from a branch.

Justus glanced back over his shoulder several times as they left. "Damn, those things are cute."

"They are." She tucked her hand under his arm as they headed for another display. "Wait until you see the penguins in the aquarium next door. They are hilarious."

"Penguins? Why would I be interested in seeing penguins? I've seen them before." He set his hand on top of hers and hauled her close to his side.

"You haven't seen anything like these before." She chuckled. She'd been to the aquarium before. The penguins were very peculiar.

"My curiosity is piqued."

They wandered through the rest of the zoo and then switched to the aquarium. After spending some time watching the giant dugongs feeding on lettuce, she led him to the penguin exhibit and they got in line. When they reached the plexiglass wall that divided the penguin habitat from the humans, she looked up at his face to see his expression.

It took a few moments, and then he laughed. "What the hell? Why are the little dudes running back and forth?"

She watched him as he glanced at the small boats as they came around the corner. "It's like a ride at Disney World. We're going to get in the little boat and ride it around to the other side through the penguin habitat."

"I see that, but what the hell are the penguins doing?" A smile was plastered on his face.

"I guess they run back and forth sort of greeting each group as they enter the boat. Isn't it adorable?" She squeezed his arm.

"It's freaky."

"That too."

# CHAPTER 7

Arianna was jumping out of her skin by the time they got back to the hotel. It was almost eight o'clock. They'd grabbed lunch on the pier and then wandered around the harbour. It felt like Justus was stalling all day. He kept pointing out places they should see, stores they should go into, views they should pause at.

When the sun went down, he'd told her he was craving a burger, so she reluctantly told him she knew exactly where the best burgers in town were. They'd headed back to Circular Quay and then made their way through the streets to the cute little corner restaurant she knew he would enjoy. The Push. They grabbed a small round bar table and ordered Dog Days Summer Ale and two burgers.

Again Justus had dragged things out. He seemed to move in slow motion. She also thought he'd been smirking for the last several hours.

"Are you in a hurry?" he asked as he opened the door to the hotel room. "You practically dragged me down the hallway." Yeah, he was laughing at her.

She spun around when they were inside, yanking her

purse over her shoulder and then shrugging out of her jacket. "I was beginning to think you didn't want to be alone with me. I half expected you to suggest dancing next, or a movie." Did she sound desperate?

He chuckled, taking her jacket and purse from her hands and setting them on the desk. "I hadn't thought of that. Should we go back out?"

She narrowed her gaze. "If you've changed your mind about us, that's fine. Just say so." It wasn't fine at all. She would be crushed. But he didn't need to know that.

He stepped closer and cupped her face. His gaze met hers. "Have you changed *your* mind?"

"No," she retorted.

His hand slid down her back to the rear pocket of her jeans where he removed her phone, turned it off, and then set it on the desk with her purse.

"You turned my phone off." She was breathless, trying to infer *anything* from his actions. He set his next to hers, though she noted he did not turn his off. She knew he couldn't. A SEAL might be granted leave to take a vacation, but they could also be recalled any time on a moment's notice.

"Yep. Surely you don't need to take a call from anyone for the next several hours."

She swallowed as he stalked her, backing up until her legs hit the edge of the bed. *Several hours?*

"I had a fun day," he murmured as he cupped her face again. "Thank you."

"You're welcome. It was long. Felt like a week."

He chuckled again. "So anxious."

She blew out a breath. She was acting ridiculous. Needy.

He threaded his fingers in her hair and held her head to one side, his lips coming down to kiss her neck and then the back of her ear. "You've been fidgeting in desperation for hours. I like it."

"If you knew that, why did you make me wait?" she breathed, reaching for his waist.

"Because it was hot. Because I wanted the desire to build. Because I wanted you to have plenty of time to change your mind." His lips hovered over her ear, nibbling around until he finally leaned back a few inches and met her gaze again.

"Not going to change my mind."

"We've spent like thirty hours together. Not even that since I slept here alone last night. Do you always decide to sleep with a man that quickly?" The question could have been serious, but his eyes were dancing with mirth. He was teasing her.

"I decided I wanted to sleep with you about a decade ago. The last thirty hours were just the home stretch."

His smile widened and then his mouth descended. He claimed her lips, rough and demanding this time. Perfect.

She fisted his T-shirt at his waist, holding on to him as if he might slip away. When his tongue slid between her lips, she opened for him. She'd been aroused all day. Her heart had been beating rapidly since she'd arrived that morning. Her nipples had been permanently stiff. Her panties soaked.

Finally. *Finally* they were here in the hotel. Alone. And he was kissing the sense out of her. If the mattress hadn't been at the back of her thighs, she might have collapsed.

By the time Justus released her lips, she was putty in his hands, gasping, needy, wanton.

He smoothed his hands down to her shoulders and held on to her, his eyes locked on hers. "No woman has ever wrapped me so tightly around her finger as you have."

She didn't move or breathe. Instead, she held his gaze.

"If we do this, we can't go back. I'm going to wear you out for nine nights."

She nodded slightly.

"And then I'm going to leave." He lifted a brow.

"I know," she whispered.

"I don't keep girlfriends, Arianna. I won't change my mind," he warned.

"I don't date military men. I won't change mine either."

He continued to stare at her for a long time, perhaps reassuring himself she was telling the truth. And then his hands went to the hem of her shirt. In a quick swoop of material, he yanked it over her head. His palms landed on her waist, his thumbs grazing the underside of her breasts, only the thin, lacy silk separating her skin from his.

She'd chosen her best panty set for today, confident this moment would eventually present itself. And here she was. She'd lusted after this man for years, daydreamed about this moment, even though until a few weeks ago, she'd never expected it to occur in her wildest imagination. And her imagination had been wild.

His gaze was on her chest. His hands smoothed up to cup her breasts, molding to them. "I've been dying to hold these all day."

She moaned when his thumbs brushed over her nipples, her grip on his shirt tightening. She'd been so aroused for so many hours that it wouldn't take much to push her over the edge. It was so unlike her. Men didn't get her this aroused, not even if they worked at it for hours. She'd always had a hard time letting herself relax and enjoy sex.

But not Justus. Her body reacted to him differently. It probably should have been frightening, but she ignored that emotion and focused on how swollen her pussy was and how much she wanted to be naked in his arms.

He seemed to be taking his time though, every action slow and meticulous. His thumbs strummed over and over her stiff nipples, driving her mad. When he dipped them under the lace and stroked bare skin, she sucked in a sharp breath and rose onto her toes.

He lifted his gaze, smiling. He released her breasts to ease his hands around to her back. Seconds later, her bra was released and fell down her arms. Justus tossed it aside.

She wanted his chest bare too, so she tugged on the fisted material. Luckily, he lifted his arms and let her drag the shirt over his head. She dropped it without looking. A whoosh of air left her mouth as he grabbed her by the waist and practically tossed her onto the bed.

Every move he made was a surprise as he switched back and forth between slow and gentle mixed with sudden sharp actions that took her breath away.

She rose onto her elbows, but quickly dropped onto her back as he crawled over her. He rested on one elbow alongside her head, leaning on his hip at her side, and slid his other hand down from her face. His gaze followed his fingers as he tortured her with a barely existent touch. Her cheek, her neck, her shoulder, her breast.

*Jesus.* He circled her nipple several times until she arched her chest toward him. Goose bumps rose all over her body. She wanted to reach for him, pull him closer, but her hands were frozen at her sides, not willing to take orders from her brain.

"I love the color of your skin," he whispered. "And the rose of your nipples. I wondered what color they would be. So sexy." Finally, he flicked his thumb over one, making her whimper.

A smile spread across his face as he met her gaze. "You're so responsive. I'm going to come in my jeans just listening to you moan."

Had she moaned? She flushed, unable to respond.

Her face grew redder because he continued to stare into her eyes as he explored her breasts with his fingers. So intense. The room was suddenly too hot.

When he slid his palm down her thigh, his thumb coming close to her sex, her vision swam. She tipped her head back, her mouth falling open. "Justus," she begged.

"Oh, I like the sound of my name coming from your lips while I make you writhe."

More heat. She was going to implode.

Finally, he rose up on his knees, popped the button of her jeans, and lowered the zipper. He slid off the bed to drag the denim and her thong down her legs, pausing only long enough to remove her shoes and socks.

When his gaze came back to hers, she felt incredibly exposed. She had on nothing while he still wore jeans. Thankfully, he kicked off his shoes and removed the rest of his clothes before she had to plead with him to do so.

His cock sprang free, thick and long, making her lick her lips.

He groaned. "You're killing me." He climbed back onto the bed, this time settling a knee between her legs. Again, he let his gaze wander all over her body while she watched. His erection bobbed in between them, but she suspected he didn't intend to use it on her yet, and her suspicion was confirmed when he dropped to one hip at her side, leaving his knee between her legs. He rested his cheek on his palm.

If he stared at every woman he took to bed like this, he surely had a slew of them pining for him all over the world. His looks would melt anyone. He didn't even need to touch her to get her wet and ready. His eyes—deep emerald pools—did all the work. His square jawline was intense, only the very corners of his lips tipped upward to cause tiny wrinkles at the edges of his eyes. She was getting used to this serious but playful look. It made her shudder.

He made things incrementally more intense by dancing his fingers over her skin. Her breasts, her belly, her thigh. When he tucked his fingers under her knee and lifted her outside leg high and wide, she bit into her lower lip.

The hairs on his thigh grazed her sex, making her hold her breath. That didn't last long, however, because he drew his hand up her thigh and between her legs. The instant his finger lightly stroked her lower lips, she gasped. She reached out with her free hand to grab his arm.

He never stopped looking into her eyes. Every time she glanced down or looked away, she found him still staring at her when she returned her gaze. With two fingers, he parted her labia, and then he slid his middle finger between the swollen folds.

She was so wet, and he dragged that moisture up to circle her clit. She gripped his arm, not trying to dislodge him, but holding on so she wouldn't fall through a crack in the universe.

"Justus…" she repeated. She didn't care if she was begging. She needed him inside her. Now.

"Mmm." He flicked her clit, and she lifted her hips, a sharp cry escaping.

"I'm gonna come," she stated unnecessarily.

"That's the idea." He smiled, straddling her clit with two fingers and using a third to flick over the swollen nub rapidly.

She sucked in a breath, her eyes rolling back, as she writhed against him. So close. So fast. Her body craved his. Inside her. He had to know that. But he didn't act on it. And she didn't have the ability to ask in words. So, she focused on his fingers instead, rising, higher, higher.

Finally, she stiffened for two seconds, those two

perfect seconds that marked the edge of sanity right before the crash. And then the pulsing as she came. She held her butt off the bed, her orgasm wracking her stiff body.

She didn't breathe or even blink until the last of the waves subsided, and then she dropped her hips and tried to focus on him. Her limbs were limp. Her hand having fallen to her side again at some point.

Still he watched her, smiling. "Damn, that was sexy."

She sucked in breaths. "You just gonna stare at me, or were you planning to fuck me?"

He smiled wider and then his fingers disappeared from her pussy and he slid off the bed. He reached for his jeans. She assumed he was going for a condom, and luckily that was the case. Ten seconds later, he was back, rolling the protection down his length and nudging her knees wider with his own.

When he lowered over her body, his cock lodged at her opening. He cupped her face and kissed her, hard. Demanding. In a heartbeat, he switched from calm and steady to rough and needy. His mouth consumed hers. His tongue tangled with hers. His lips shifted back and forth as if he couldn't decide exactly how he wanted to kiss her but intended to try every single angle in the fewest seconds possible.

His chest rubbed over her nipples, bringing them to attention. He used his knees to press hers wider.

God, she wanted him inside her. Now. Holy shit. *Now.*

Finally, he broke the kiss. He was gasping for air as he stared at her once again. "Fast or slow?"

"Fast." She grabbed his hips and slid her hands around to his ass, wrapping her legs around his waist. "Jesus, Justus, fast. Do it."

He thrust into her in the next instant. All the way. Deep

and thorough. The base of him flat against her tormented pussy.

The air rushed from her lungs. He was so damn big. He filled her like no one ever had. And she loved it. She wanted more.

She could no longer focus enough to know if he was still watching her, but then he gritted his teeth as if it took every ounce of willpower to keep from moving.

But she didn't want him to avoid moving. She wanted him to fuck her.

She bucked her hips the most miniscule amount possible. "Justus," she cried out, her fingers digging into his butt.

He pulled out and thrust back in, the air whooshing from his lungs. As if there was no way he could continue to hold himself above her, he lowered his chest to hers and set his forehead on the mattress next to her. And then he really moved. In and out. Hard, rapid thrusts that drove her arousal back where it had been before she came.

That had only been a minute ago. How the hell could she be this close to the edge again? It wasn't possible. But it was. Every time the base of his cock slammed into her clit, she gasped.

Surprising her, he lifted his face to hers again, held himself up with one elbow, and slid his other hand down her body to worm between their bellies. When his fingers stroked her clit, she knew she was going to come again.

His face was tight. He was holding back.

Her mouth fell open.

He kept pumping. In and out. Still so hard. Every nerve ending inside her came to life. Demanding more.

"Come for me, Arianna," he demanded.

As if it were that simple, she came, her tight channel squeezing around him in a different sort of orgasm from any she'd ever had before. More intense. More of everything.

He groaned loudly and held himself deep inside her, his hand coming away from her clit to help hold him up. She could feel the pulses of his orgasm as his entire body rocked forward with every wave.

It lasted forever, and then he collapsed to his side, taking her with him, his cock still lodged inside her warmth. His hand came up to her face, and he kissed her so very gently. And then he gave a slow grin. "See, I can do soft and sweet."

She giggled. "But rough and demanding is so nice."

# CHAPTER 8

When Justus awoke late the next morning to find Arianna staring down at him, he groaned and then rolled onto his side and buried his head in his pillow.

She laughed from behind him and leaned into his back to kiss his shoulder. "What was that you were telling me yesterday? Oh, right. I remember. You said you would never be able to sleep soundly enough for me to stare at you."

He grumbled, and then he flipped over, taking her by surprise, to flatten her on her back and hover over her. "How long have you been awake?" he asked as he threaded his fingers in her hair and held her head to one side so he could kiss her neck.

She squirmed. "Not long. Someone wore me out."

He lifted his face and waggled his brows at her. "Then I win, because I watched you sleep for hours."

She scrunched up her cute nose. "That must have been boring."

He cupped her face and stroked her cheek with his

thumb. "I enjoyed it." He glanced down. "You're wearing my shirt."

She shrugged. "I'm not used to being naked. I felt...naked."

He bolted to sitting, grabbed the hem, and tugged it over her head. "I happen to like naked."

God, she was gorgeous. As he stared at her nipples, they stiffened and she shivered. He cupped her breast and leaned down to flick his tongue over one distended tip. "What time does our agenda begin today?"

"Hmm. I thought we'd skip my original plan to walk on the beach, spend the day in bed, and then hit a brewery tour tonight."

"I like that plan. Isn't it kind of cold for the beach?"

"I didn't say we were going to sunbathe. But the Bondi Beach is a beautiful walk that shouldn't be missed."

"Can we do it when we get back in town?"

"Yep."

"Then let's go with your new plan. Sex. Room service. Beer."

"Who mentioned sex?"

As it turned out, sex turned into more sex, and room service didn't happen until about noon. By the time they arrived for the first leg of their brewery tour, they were both famished, and in need of fresh air. Luckily, the first stop included local pizza, which was divine.

Arianna was smiling, her body still humming, when they met up with their guide and began drinking.

Justus never stopped staring her. And he always had a hand on the small of her back when they were standing, her thigh if they were sitting. The other people in their group kept grinning at them as if they were newlyweds.

It was bittersweet since Arianna felt fairly confident the feelings she had this evening were stronger than most newlyweds ever felt. Perhaps it was simply the newness of the relationship, that stage where it felt like your partner was perfect before you knew enough about him or her to take a step back.

Except something was different. It was more. No man had ever made her feel this alive. She feared no other man ever would. Already on their third day together she worried about what would happen when he left her.

What if she fell in too deep? She couldn't let that happen. She needed to harden her heart and not let it fall too far. They both agreed. She didn't date military men, and he didn't date because he was in the military.

Reasonable. Rational. Understandable.

Now, she just needed to keep her heart out of it.

They moved to their second stop, another pub—except she'd quickly learned months ago that in Australia bars were called hotels. And their current tour guide explained how that term came to be. Apparently, years ago, the only way for a place to serve alcohol was if it also had at least one bed for overnight guests. Thus, every location that served drinks had to be a hotel. It stuck and the term was still in use today.

The tour guide was entertaining too. Everyone was intrigued when he explained in great detail how this second location claimed to be the oldest hotel in Sydney. Apparently there were three such locations, and the distinctions were interesting. There was the oldest one still in the same location, the oldest one by name even though it had once burned down and was now rebuilt, and the oldest one still using the same name though it had moved locations.

Justus seemed to be having a great time. At each stop, they tried the local microbrews. The history was fascinating, and even though Australia was nearly the same age as the United States, there seemed to be an incredible amount of preserved history in the heart of Sydney.

When they finished the tour and parted from the other visitors, Justus threaded his fingers with hers and led her randomly down the brick sidewalks. "It's beautiful here. Even at night." He lifted his gaze to take in the Harbour Bridge in the background. "I heard you can climb the outside of the bridge to the top. Is that true?"

"Yes. If we walk closer during the day, you'll be able to see groups of people in blue coveralls climbing the steps along the top of the bridge. They wear elaborate harnesses."

He released her hand and wrapped his arm around her waist, pulling her to his side. "You didn't include this on our itinerary?" he teased.

She lifted her face. "Not a chance in hell, but if you want to do it, we can make it happen. I just won't be doing it with you."

He laughed. She loved the sound of his deep laughter, doubting that in his regular life he often let himself relax and enjoy anything enough to express that much emotion. She knew Tony didn't. It always took him several days when he returned from a deployment to even smile, let alone laugh.

Suddenly, Justus stopped walking. Arianna lifted her gaze to find him staring at the ground. He released her and bent down to pick something up. When he stood, he was holding an enormous diamond ring. If it was real.

"Holy shit," she whispered, glancing around. How the hell could someone have lost something like that? Even if it was cubic zirconia. It still had to be valuable. The gold setting was stunning, the center diamond surrounded by several smaller ones in an oval pattern.

Justus narrowed his gaze, scrutinizing the ring closer.

"You think it's real?"

"I don't know. But if it is, someone's surely very upset. This has to be worth more money than I'll see in my lifetime."

"What should we do?"

"Let's take it to the police station. I can't think of anything else."

Arianna pulled her phone out of her back pocket and used the map, learning that the closest station was only a few blocks away. "We can easily walk from here."

Justus put the ring on his pinky and tucked it into his palm, hurrying her through the streets as if they were suddenly unsafe. He didn't relax until they were inside the station. The man at the entrance desk glanced at the ring and then made a call to someone else in the station.

Within minutes, they were ushered behind the front entrance in an open room that contained several desks. Most were unoccupied, but a few had officers. One of them stood and waved them over. He extended his hand. "I'm Officer Stanton. I understand you found a ring?" He pointed at the two seats across from his desk, and Justus took one while Arianna took the other.

Justus held out the ring, handing it to the officer. "No idea if it's real, but it appears to be very intricate, so someone must be frantic if it's an actual diamond."

The officer lifted it closer. "It's real, all right. The owner reported it stolen two weeks ago. Where did you find it?"

"Lying in the dirt next to the sidewalk about two blocks from here," Arianna told him. "I can show you where on a map." She opened her phone, scanned in closer to the location, and pointed to the spot.

"Was this the only thing you found?" The officer's eyes were narrowed in concern. For the first time since they'd located the ring, Arianna's skin crawled. It seemed like he didn't believe them. What if he thought they'd stolen it?

"Yes," Justus responded. "I glanced around. I didn't see anything else. It was angled just right so that the lights coming from the harbour caught it."

The officer glanced back and forth between the two of them. "Are you on holiday?"

Justus nodded. "I am. I arrived two days ago. I'm a Navy SEAL on leave. Arianna is here for the year on a work-and-holiday visa."

The officer hesitated, his actions again making Arianna stiffen. It was too bad regular people couldn't do a simple good deed without being suspect, but perhaps she needed to be more understanding under the circumstances.

Finally, Officer Stanton gave them a brief nod. "There was a home break-in not far from where you found this ring. Perhaps even across the street. An enormous amount of jewelry was seized. Were you aware there was a reward posted for the return of this ring? It's a family heirloom."

Justus sat up straighter beside Arianna. He rubbed his thighs with both hands. "We had no idea. Nor are we interested in any reward. We simply wanted to return the ring to its owner."

Stanton sat back, rubbing his chin. "I need to call the owner. Can you wait here a moment, please?"

"Of course."

The officer stood and made his way across the room,

taking the ring with him. He went through a door and disappeared.

Arianna was shaking. She glanced around. There were a few people sitting against a wall behind her. They looked rough and pissed, as if they'd been brought in for some variety of charges and were awaiting processing. She rubbed her arms as she yanked her gaze back to Justus. "I'm not sure he believes us."

Justus pursed his lips, his brows rising. "I'm not sure he does either, but what the hell else were we supposed to do?"

They sat in silence for a few minutes, and then the officer returned. "The owner is on her way to the station now."

"I see." Justus looked concerned. "Do you need us to make a statement or something?"

Arianna opened her purse and pulled out their folded itinerary. She opened it and handed it to Stanton. "This is our itinerary for the next week." She hoped if she provided him with all their details, he wouldn't detain them. The last thing she wanted to do was spend hours in this damn police station being questioned about a ring they found.

Stanton glanced at the paper. "You're heading to Cairns tomorrow."

"Yes." She nodded, hoping this wasn't going to escalate into a problem that derailed their plans.

He glanced at the paper. "Good. Your cell is on here in case I need to reach you. Do you have documentation with you? Passports?"

She pulled a copy of her passport out of her purse and handed it to the officer.

"My passport is in the hotel," Justus stated. "I put it in the safe."

"Not a problem. As long as I have one, I'll be able to

find you if I have any more questions." He stood again. "Give me a second to photocopy this."

Justus ran a hand down his face as Arianna watched Stanton cross the room.

Voices came from behind them, and when Stanton returned, he had an older woman and a man closer to their age with him. The woman wore a cream-colored blouse and a tweed skirt. She had a pale pink sweater draped over her shoulders and a hand plastered to her chest. She looked the part of someone wealthy enough to own such a ring.

She held out a hand. "I'm Bernice Parker. I understand you found my wedding ring?"

Arianna stood at the same time as Justus. Justus shook the woman's hand. "I have no idea, ma'am. Perhaps. We found it next to the sidewalk while we were walking."

Stanton handed Bernice a sealed plastic bag in which the ring now rested.

Bernice took it with shaking fingers. Tears ran down her face. "My God," she murmured. "I never thought I'd see this again in my lifetime."

Arianna smiled. This was why they'd come to the police. They'd made this woman's day. The man next to her took the ring next and brought it closer to his face. "It looks like your lucky day, Mum." He handed it back, beaming.

"Jerry, write these people a check, would you?"

The man named Jerry pulled a checkbook from his back pocket.

Arianna opened her mouth to protest, but Justus beat her to it. "No." He held out a hand. "Please. We don't want any reward. We're just glad the ring made it back to its owner. That's reward enough."

Jerry ignored Justus, leaning over Stanton's desk as he scribbled on the check.

"Seriously," Arianna added, stepping closer. She grabbed Justus's arm and met Bernice's gaze. "We don't want your money. Stanton said there were other things stolen? Save the reward for someone else. Maybe you'll get lucky and other pieces will be found."

Bernice wiped her eyes, holding the ring close to her heart. She shook her head. "Nearly all of my jewelry was stolen that day. None of it was as valuable to me as this ring."

Justus set a hand gently on Bernice's arm. "I'm so glad you got it back, ma'am, but we can't take your money."

"You must. I posted a reward. And I always keep my word."

Arianna leaned closer again. "We didn't know anything about your reward, though, so there is no need."

Bernice set a shaky hand on Arianna's cheek. "You're such a dear child." She smiled, tears still falling. "Thank you for being so gracious, but you must. I wouldn't be able to sleep if I didn't reward you two." Her gaze went to Justus. She smiled. "Are you on your honeymoon?"

Justus smiled back. "No, ma'am. We haven't known each other that long."

Bernice glanced back and forth between them. Her smile widened. "Well, I can tell you are perfect for each other. Such a lovely couple. You look so in love." She glanced at where Arianna held on to Justus's arm. "I remember when I used to grip my Willard that way, God rest his soul. It's been so many years since we were your age."

Arianna choked up. No wonder the ring meant so much to her. Her husband had passed.

Jerry folded the check in half and handed it to Justus.

He held Justus's gaze. "Trust me. There's no sense arguing with my mother. She doesn't take no for an answer. She's got more money than she knows what to do with. Please, just take the check. If you don't, I'll have to listen to her fretting for weeks. It will make her rest easier knowing you were rewarded."

Justus nodded slowly. "Okay, then." He slid the check into his pocket without looking at it.

Stanton cleared his throat. "You two are free to go. I've got your information if I have any further questions." He held up the wrinkled piece of paper and then set it on his desk to follow all of them toward the front entrance.

When they stepped outside, Justus took Arianna's hand and held it tighter than usual. He thanked Bernice and Jerry again, shook both their hands, and wished them happiness.

Arianna was still too shook up to speak. She let Justus lead her down the street without saying a word. It wasn't until they were back in the hotel room that Justus took the check out of his pocket and unfolded it. "Holy shit," he exclaimed, so loudly the people in both flanking rooms could surely hear him.

Arianna removed her jacket and draped it over the desk chair. "I take it it's a lot?" She came to him and slid it from his hand. Her eyes bugged out. "No way," she stammered.

"Give me your phone." Justus held out his hand.

She pulled it from her pocket and handed it to him, knowing it would be easier for him to place a call from her Australian number than his international one.

He paced away from her, holding the officer's card while he dialed.

Arianna dropped to sit on the bed as she watched Justus rub his forehead and finally speak. "Yes, Officer Stanton. This is Justus Kirkland... Yes, that's right. This check. We can't accept this... I understand... No... But..." There was a long silence on their end when Arianna assumed Stanton was speaking. The expression on Justus's face was pained. "That's crazy. This is a lot of money... I know, but..." Finally, he sighed, his shoulders dropping. "Okay... Yes... Fine." He ended the call and stared at Arianna. "I guess our vacation just kicked it up a notch."

## CHAPTER 9

A notch was the understatement of the century. There was no way Justus was going to be able to sleep with this check in the room. He also knew he wasn't the only one freaking out. It disturbed him that they'd walked so casually back to the hotel room with that amount of money scribbled on a piece of paper loose in his pocket.

After they took turns using the bathroom and changing, they climbed into bed, Arianna in one of his T-shirts like he'd found her that morning, him in a pair of flannel pants. He flopped onto his back and pulled her against his chest, kissing the top of her head.

"You think we should try to return it again tomorrow?" she asked, her fingers trailing across his chest.

"I don't think it will do any good. The woman was adamant. It might even hurt her feelings."

Arianna sighed against him. "What the hell do we do next?"

"You've got a bank account here, right?" He tipped his head down toward her.

"Of course, but I usually deposit a few hundred dollars

at a time. Nothing like that." She lifted a concerned gaze to his, setting her chin on his chest.

"Well, it's our only option. We can't just carry it around. We'll deposit it in your account first thing in the morning."

She shoved off him and sat cross-legged next to him. "It's not mine. If it belongs to anyone, it should be you. I didn't even see the ring."

He reached for her face and stroked her cheek. "What the hell would I do with it? I don't need money. I'm a SEAL. I don't even own things. All the money I've made for nine years is already just sitting in a bank collecting dust. That's why I can take elaborate vacations like this." He tucked a strand of hair behind her ear and slid his hand down to her back, urging her forward.

She resisted. "Justus, no." She flattened her palms on his chest. "I can put the money in my account for safekeeping if you want, but it's yours, not mine. I know you don't have siblings, but don't you have cousins with kids or something? Open a college account."

He laughed. "I have one cousin. She has two small kids. No one is going to college anytime soon."

"Well, your own kids, then."

He laughed harder. "I'm not having kids. I don't even want a girlfriend."

She stiffened, closing her eyes for a moment, and then she wiggled free of him and padded toward the bathroom. She stayed in there for a while, the water running.

He stared at the door, breathing deeply. Perhaps his words hadn't been well thought out, but she knew this thing between them wasn't permanent. She had no reason to be pissed just because he'd pointed out something they'd already agreed on. A fling. If she couldn't do this, then they needed to part ways now.

He pushed to sitting, leaning against the headboard.

When she returned, she crawled back onto the bed and kneeled next to him. She met his gaze dead on. "Sorry. I needed a moment. You're absolutely right. We'll take the money to my bank in the morning for safe keeping. When you get back to the States, I'll wire transfer you half of it. Fair?"

He smiled, relieved she didn't mention their relationship status. "Fair," he agreed.

She returned the smile and crawled over his lap, straddling him. She pressed her warm core against his cock and cupped his face. "We good?"

"I am. You?"

She nodded. "Definitely."

"Still on the same page?" he asked, needing to be sure.

"Definitely," she repeated.

That was when he grabbed the hem of his T-shirt and hauled it over her head. He cupped her breasts and flicked his thumbs over her nipples because he'd quickly learned the act made her lose her mind every time.

She moaned, leaning her head back as her eyes slid closed. "God, you drive me wild."

"Good. It's sexy as hell." He reached toward the bedside table with one hand and snagged a condom, one of the dozen he'd purchased the previous afternoon. They were going to have to replace them soon at the rate they were going.

After easing her back a few inches farther down his thighs, he lifted his hips, tugged his sleep pants over his cock, and rolled on the condom. Almost before he could get his hands out of the way, Arianna rose above his erection and slammed down, burying him to the hilt.

He groaned, his hands going to her hips. "Baby…" The word slipped out. An endearment that probably wasn't appropriate between them. But it was too late.

She lifted and resettled several more times, her head falling back, her neck elongated.

He kissed the exposed length of skin, loving the feel of her neck against his lips, the scent of her body, the way she gripped his cock with her channel. God, he loved everything about her.

He froze, squeezing his eyes shut, grateful all those thoughts had remained inside and not been spoken out loud. He'd used the four-letter word flippantly in his mind, like anyone would refer to an ice cream or their dream car. Still, he needed to watch it. This was a temporary arrangement. Nothing more.

When Arianna reached between their bodies to stroke her clit, he nearly came instantly. He watched her movements, focusing his attention on the way she liked to be touched, forcing his dick to stand down long enough to enjoy the view and watch her come before him.

It didn't take long. When her breathing changed to short pants and her head fell forward, he slid his fingers down to meet hers and stroked her clit simultaneously. Seconds later, she came. He could feel the pulsing of her tight pussy around his cock. She hesitated only a few seconds as the first waves washed through her, and then she removed her hand from between them, grabbed his shoulders, and bounced up and down on his dick.

Her breasts swayed with the movements, enticing him, luring him closer. In less than a minute, he was there, grabbing her hips to plant her down firmly on his erection as waves of his orgasm washed through him.

Arianna smiled as she stared down at a very sleeping, dead-to-the-world Justus. She had been awake for half an hour, but she hadn't moved except to prop her head on her elbow and watched his face at peace. He was on his stomach, arms above his head, tucked under his pillow, facing her.

The sheet had slid down low enough for her to take in his amazing back. She admired the tattoos that extended down his biceps and the one between shoulder blades. They were intricate and well-done. A trident adorned one arm. The names of fallen comrades draped down the other arm. An American flag stretched between his shoulder blades. That one was in full vibrant color.

She longed to trace the edges with her fingers, but didn't dare. Their flight to Cairns wasn't until later that afternoon. They had all morning. He was obviously still disoriented from either the time change or sleep deprivation. He had not only flown from Los Angeles to Sydney, but before that he'd gone from South Africa to Los Angeles.

She felt confident he'd only fallen asleep a few hours before, as he had the previous nights, so she didn't want to disturb him. He was on vacation. There was no reason to wake him. And the view for her was not too shabby.

Damn, he was sexy. Even asleep. Especially asleep. Full lips parted. His brow smooth. He was one of the lucky ones. She had no idea what he'd witnessed in combat, but it didn't appear that he suffered from PTSD or night terrors. So many military personnel did.

Though the sheet had slid down to his fantastic ass, she, luckily, had her side tucked up under her arms. She hadn't put on one of his T-shirts. If she moved, she would risk waking him.

What would it be like to wake up next to this man for the rest of her life? It wasn't an option, of course, but she could dream. One more week was all she would have. He would return to the other side of the earth to fight evil. She would continue her work in Australia and then return to New York.

Her ten days with him would forever be nothing more than a blip in time. Another life. Something she would cherish forever. She closed her eyes and silently rolled to her back, inhaling slowly. A new concern she had never considered crept into her psyche.

How would another man ever take Justus's place?

She'd dated enough men and had enough short-term boyfriends to know this thing with Justus was different. No one had ever looked at her the way he did. No one had ever touched her as gently, nor as reverently. No one had ever made her feel a constant tingle, one that grabbed her soul and held her tight.

When he left, there would be an emptiness. Perhaps much larger than she'd anticipated when she proposed this arrangement. And she suspected he felt the same way, based on the way he stared at her and how attentive he was.

It wasn't as though they could renegotiate even if they both agreed, because the facts remained. He lived in a world far away from hers, both emotionally and physically. She didn't have the strength to commit to a man she would see for no more than a few weeks a year. She wanted more than that. She wanted the world.

She'd known from a young age that she would never marry someone in the military, or even date one out of fear she might fall for him. And she'd stuck to that personal rule.

One of her favorite aunts on her mother's side was married to a marine. She'd raised four kids on her own, shedding many a tear at Arianna's kitchen table when she thought only her sister was in hearing range.

In the end, after fifteen years of service, her husband was killed in combat. It was one of the most horrifying childhood experiences Arianna could remember. She'd been about eight when he died, and that was the day she swore she would never put herself in a position to feel that kind of pain and loss.

Arianna worried this vacation was a terrible mistake. Every hour she spent with Justus drew her closer to him. Every moment was precious. Would she survive the inevitable end?

She took a deep breath, opened her eyes, and rolled back to face him, knowing there was no way in hell she would drive him away. She would take these remaining days and make every second count. They had to be enough for a lifetime.

Even if she lost her heart to him, she could always fall back on that old phrase: *Better to have loved and lost than never to have loved at all*. Maybe it didn't fit this scenario. Maybe that lesson was meant to imply that they should stick together after this vacation and take their chances.

But, no. No matter how deep she fell for him, it would be easier in the long run to stick to the plan. Cut all ties. Move on with her life. Find a man who could not only love her but do so inside the same house.

Was it possible to be ruined for all other men?

"I can practically hear you thinking," Justus murmured without moving a muscle other than one corner of his lips. He had one eye open.

She flinched. "Jesus, you scared me."

He slowly rolled to his side, facing her, his hand coming to her hip. "You were so lost inside your head there was no way to avoid startling you."

"I wasn't lost," she lied, leaning closer to kiss his shoulder. Now that he was awake, she wanted to touch him. Everywhere. She held back the urge, not wanting to seem so eager.

Shocking her, his hand on her hip suddenly snaked around to her back, and he hauled her body forward until she was flush against him.

She gasped, her hands going to his shoulders.

"That's better." His face was lazy and still half asleep, his eyes hooded, his lips coming to hers. He nibbled around her mouth and cheek and neck and ear until she squirmed. "What time do we have to be at the airport?" he whispered, his breath making her shiver.

"Three."

"Plenty of time then." His tongue reached out to tease the sensitive skin behind her ear.

"For what?" she joked, tipping her head back to give him better access.

"To make it to the bank, of course." He chuckled.

She smiled. "I don't think that will take long."

"True. And on top of everything else, I say we order room service, possibly for the rest of our meals. After all, it would seem we can afford it. Might as well live it up."

"I say we deposit the money but take out several hundred-dollar bills and hand them to people who look like they need it as we travel."

He leaned back and met her gaze, holding it for several seconds before speaking. "You're an amazing woman."

"Thank you."

# CHAPTER 10

"Keep that purse across your shoulder at all times," Justus whispered close to her ear as the two of them slid onto bar stools at their hotel in Cairns.

"I will. Don't worry." She didn't think it was all that necessary. After all, if someone was so desperate that they stole her purse, they probably needed the contents more than either her or Justus, but she knew he cared more about her safety than anything else.

"What do you want to drink?" he asked as the bartender came over.

"Choose me a local beer."

"Easy enough." While he consulted with the bartender, a man slid onto the stool next to Arianna. He dropped a backpack on the floor next to his stool with a thump and sighed.

She smiled in his direction to be polite. "Long day?"

He glanced at her, seemingly shocked to realize someone was even next to him. "You have no idea. More like long life."

She scrunched up her face. "Sorry to hear that. Can we

buy you a beer? Might not fix your problems, but it will take the edge off."

He smirked. "Sure. Why not?"

Arianna turned toward the bartender just as Justus finished ordering. "Add his beer to our tab," she said, nodding to the newcomer.

"You got it."

Justus leaned around the front of Arianna and extended a hand. "Justus Kirkland."

The man took his hand. "Chris Metz."

"This is my girlfriend, Arianna," Justus said by way of introduction as he settled a hand around her waist possessively.

She smiled at him, her heart pounding. He'd made it perfectly clear that he didn't do girlfriends, never wanted one, and she was certainly not one. She knew his words were pure posturing, a way for him to lay claim to her and ensure no one else got any ideas. Never mind that the claim was for seven more days.

"Nice to meet you both," Chris responded, his voice despondent.

"He's having a bad day, or, uh, life," Arianna informed Justus.

"Ah," was Justus's response.

The bartender set their beers on the counter and walked away as three other customers arrived at the other end of the bar.

Arianna lifted her glass high. "To better days."

The men flanking her clinked glasses with hers.

"Trying to place your accent," Justus commented. "You're not from Australia, right?"

Arianna agreed. Though he wasn't from the US either. Nor was he from England.

"New Zealand."

"What brings you to Cairns?" Arianna asked conversationally. He seemed nice enough, even if his eyes seemed to suggest his entire family had recently died in a car crash. He was shorter than Justus, maybe five-ten. Skinny. Dark hair. Pale skin. An ordinary sort of guy that didn't stand out as being particularly good-looking or otherwise. At least for her.

"I'm on my honeymoon actually, except my fiancée didn't show up for the wedding, so I've come on my own." He didn't look at them as he spoke. Instead, he ran a finger around the rim of his beer glass.

Arianna cringed. "I'm so sorry. How awful."

Chris shrugged. "What can you do? I figured I would make the most of the trip we had planned anyway. Too bad Shelly wiped out the checking account and maxed out the credit cards before she took off, a fact I did not know until I arrived in Cairns and handed my credit card to the hotel desk clerk."

"Yikes." Arianna's first thought was, *Hey, a guy we can help!* But Justus's grip on her waist made her hesitate. Something about the way he stiffened made her think he disagreed, so she glanced at him.

He was frowning and subtly shaking his head. Why? Hadn't they just that morning taken out cash to help out random strangers throughout the trip?

She turned back to Chris. "You don't even know where she went?"

He shook his head. "No idea. We've been together for a year. We already had a joint account." He ran a hand through his hair, not meeting Arianna's gaze. "It's like she swindled me."

Justus stiffened again.

Arianna spun her head toward him, eyes open wide in question. *What?* Chris's story sounded so pitiful. He was just a random guy in a hotel bar. Why the hell would he be lying?

"Dude, that sucks," Justus offered. He slid his hand from around Arianna's waist and grabbed her hand, holding it on the bar between them. He didn't thread their fingers together like he usually did. Instead, he placed his palm over the back of her hand and wrapped his fingers around her much smaller ones. He casually took a sip of his beer.

Arianna took a long drink too.

Chris stared down at his beer, playing with the condensation.

"Can we get a couple of appetizers?" Arianna asked the bartender when he came by.

"Sure." He handed her a menu.

Arianna ignored the fact that Justus wouldn't release her hand when she tugged, using her free hand to hold the menu and then point at a few easy things that could be shared between three people. Surely Justus wouldn't find fault with that.

She was apparently wrong, since he drew in a deep breath only she could hear and held it too long. She didn't bother looking at him this time. Instead, slightly miffed, she spoke to Chris again. "At least you got the vacation," she offered, sounding lame. "Might as well enjoy it."

"Yep." He sat up straighter, turned to face her, and pasted on a smile.

For a few minutes, they all three sat in silence, drinking their beers. The bartender brought the appetizers and three small plates. He set a pile of napkins on the bar and took away Chris's empty glass.

"Can we get another round, please?" Arianna asked. Her fingers were starting to hurt from Justus squeezing them over and over, so she finally yanked her hand free and dramatically flexed it. *Jesus.* What the hell was wrong with him?

"What do you do for a living?" she asked Chris nonchalantly.

"Construction," he answered quickly.

Arianna swore Justus groaned. It was almost embarrassing. She decided it was best to speed this along and get to their room before Justus said something rude. She'd never seen him like this. It was a side of him she didn't recognize.

To fill the space, she told Chris about her education and her job in Sydney. She left out anything about Justus since he obviously thought she was loony.

When she reached for her purse, intending to pay the bill, Justus swatted her hand away and gave the bartender a credit card.

Chris pulled out his wallet, took out a few bills, and reached around Arianna to hand them to Justus.

Thank God Justus waved him off. "I got it, man."

"You sure? I don't mean to take advantage of you."

"Not a problem at all." He slid off the chair and reached for Arianna's waist. "We wish you all the luck. So sorry to hear about your fiancée."

"Thanks." Chris smiled. "You folks have a nice holiday."

Arianna practically had to jog to keep up with Justus as he ushered her from the room with a hand on the small of her back. It wasn't until they were in the elevator that she turned to him and put her hands on her hips. "What the fuck, Justus?"

Justus sighed and rubbed his temples. "Arianna, he was full of shit."

She leaned toward him, eyes widening. "Why the hell do you think that?"

"Because I'm good at reading people."

She shook her head. "You're paranoid. That's what you are. We've never seen that man in our lives. We just got to Cairns an hour ago. Why would some stranger randomly sit next to us in a nice hotel hoping to scam us? Not a single person in the entire northeastern part of this country even knows I have any money in my purse at all." Her voice was rising, and she snapped her mouth shut when the elevator opened.

Justus held the door open with a hand to the sensor while she exited the elevator. He followed her down the hallway and then opened their room with the keycard. As soon as they were inside, he kicked off his shoes as he responded. "I didn't say it made sense. I said I got a bad vibe from him."

She dropped her purse on the desk and spun around to face him, hands on her hips again. "And I say you're being irrationally paranoid."

He shrugged. "Maybe. But I couldn't help how the hairs on the back of my neck stood on end." He slowly stepped toward her, blowing out a breath. When he reached her, he set his hands on her waist and tugged her playfully closer, forcing a small conciliatory smile. "I'm sorry. Perhaps I overreacted. The guy rubbed me wrong."

She set her hands on his chest, wondering if there was significant merit to his intuition. After all, he was a trained Navy SEAL. She was not. Maybe she should listen to him. "I'm sorry too. I didn't mean to be so contrary. I'm just not nearly as mistrustful as you."

He lowered his face and set his forehead against hers. "I'm not usually. I swear. Just something about that guy. I doubt his name is even Chris Metz."

"Well, it's over now. At least we bought him a few beers. We'll never see him again."

"Exactly." Justus smiled, easing his hands around to her

back and then down to cup her ass. "Maybe I can lure your clothes off with the promise of a backrub."

She slowly grinned. "Perhaps…"

Justus couldn't explain his intuition, but his radar had gone on full alert the second that man had settled on the stool next to Arianna. Why the hell had the guy chosen a stool right next to a woman who was clearly with another man when there were so many open seats in the bar? Right off the bat, that had raised Justus's hackles. It had gone from bad to worse when he stammered out his sob story.

Maybe Arianna was right. Maybe Justus had been overreacting. But he was not usually wrong when it came to judging people around him even before they opened their mouths.

Several things didn't add up. Construction? Not a chance in hell. The guy didn't look fit enough to lift a book, let alone heavy equipment. And who had such a complete lack of knowledge about their personal finances that they made it all the way to the destination before realizing they don't have funds?

As Justus slowly undressed Arianna, hoping to make her forget the strange guy, he wondered if he had simply been pissed off because it seemed the man was flirting with Arianna who was clearly with Justus.

And where the hell had this jealous streak come from? A random stranger in a bar managed to grab her attention and had him acting like a caveman. No way was Justus threatened by this Chris guy, but he still found he didn't like other people capturing her attention. As if he had some sort of claim on her.

Arianna had her bottom lip tucked between her teeth

when Justus dropped her shirt on the floor and went for the zipper on her jeans. He prayed he could restore the peace between them quickly. He did not want to argue with her for even a single moment.

Their clock was ticking. He wanted to enjoy her. He kicked himself, knowing there would have been no harm in letting her give that guy money. She would have been pleased, and Justus would not now be trying to get her to forget they ever met Chris Metz.

What would it have hurt? So what if the guy swindled Arianna out of a few hundred dollars? Who cared, if it kept the peace?

He crouched down in front of her to tug her jeans down her legs.

She set her hands on his shoulders and lifted first one foot and then the other, letting him remove the denim.

With his face level with her sweet center, he decided not to rise just yet. Instead, he held her hips and pressed his nose against the thin layer of silk that covered her mound. He inhaled her fantastic scent.

She held his shoulders tighter, her fingers digging into his muscles delightfully. Since she didn't seem intent on denying him, he dragged his tongue along the edge of her panties.

She moaned. There was a god. "I thought there was a massage involved in this…" she murmured.

He chuckled and rose to his feet, releasing her. "There is. Absolutely." He pulled his shirt over his head and then backed her up toward the king-sized bed.

She'd made reservations everywhere they were planning to go. When they arrived, he'd upgraded them to a much better room on a higher floor. Why not?

When the backs of her knees hit the mattress, he spun

her around and swatted her ass playfully. "Up. Lie on your stomach."

She glanced over her shoulder as she crawled on her hands and knees toward the center of the bed. Her lip was still between her teeth, but she was fighting a smile.

He left her to get situated and padded to the bathroom to grab the hotel lotion. It was the only thing at his disposal, so it would have to do. When he returned, he found her naked, her arms above her head hugging a pillow. She'd discarded her bra and panties.

*Again, thank you, God.*

Justus removed his jeans, but left his boxer briefs on. He joined her, straddling her thighs as he squeezed the lotion onto his palm. And then he set his hands on her smooth back. Her skin never ceased to amaze him. Her Italian heritage gave her the most gorgeous skin tone he'd ever seen. Against his lighter combination of Scottish and Irish skin, she looked ravishing.

She groaned deeply when he massaged her shoulders, digging his fingers into her tight muscles.

He breathed a sigh of relief, knowing she would forgive him for his ridiculous behavior. As he continued, working his way down her back and then her ass, he scooted farther down her body. Eventually he added the backs of her thighs, pressing his fingertips into her warm flesh, while letting his thumbs graze precariously close to her sex.

Her moans of pleasure changed, and he watched her fist her hands in the pillow.

Finally, he smoothed his hands back up her body, giving her one last squeeze at her shoulders, and then he leaned over her, lowered his mouth to her ear, and whispered, "I'm sorry for earlier. I don't know what came over me."

She flipped over onto her back between his planted

hands and knees. Facing him now, she licked her lips. "Forgiven. Now, please, please, please make love to me."

"Gladly." He shrugged out of his briefs, grabbed a condom, and climbed between her legs as she spread them. Knowing she would not need any further preparation, he thrust into her to the hilt.

She grabbed his biceps and cried out. "God, I love it when you do that."

"Do what? Rough and demanding?" he teased.

"Yessss." The word came out on a hiss because he'd pulled out and was thrusting back into her as she tried to speak.

Damn, he was into her. Probably too into her. She was everything. The entire package. If he had to make a list of attributes that encompassed the perfect woman, she would easily come out ahead of anyone he'd ever dated.

Lust? Maybe. But he worried it was more than that. And he couldn't do more. He wouldn't.

Closing his eyes, he tried to focus only on how good it felt to be enveloped inside her without the added bonus of looking into her eyes or even soaking in her features. The combination was too much for him at the moment.

Every passing day drew him closer to her. Even the naïve way she trusted whoever that man was at the bar endeared him to her.

He was in over his head with this woman. Tony's sister. Gah.

# CHAPTER 11

They were on the Skyrail Rainforest Cableway, slowly inching above the Barron Gorge National Park. Arianna hadn't been to Queensland yet, so she was mesmerized by the rainforest below. "This is so beautiful."

Justus sat next to her, his body turned toward her, his hand on her back. "It is."

Another couple sat across from them, equally mesmerized. They'd introduced themselves briefly and said they were from Ohio, but all four of them were too in awe of the scenery to make small talk.

"I'm glad the weather cleared," Justus continued. It had rained earlier in the morning.

"Me too. *Look*." She pointed at the top of a tree as they passed within a few feet of it. A large bird sat on one of the uppermost branches. Regal. Gorgeous.

Justus ran his hand up and down her back. He set his chin on her shoulder. It seemed as though he'd been more attentive since they left Chris in the bar, silently begging forgiveness she rationalized. He didn't need to. There was nothing to forgive. It was over. Done. It didn't matter who was right. They would never know.

It took a long time to reach the Kuranda Terminal at the top of the mountain, and then they disembarked and wandered down a long street filled with tourist attractions. Shops that boasted all types of souvenirs.

Justus pointed down a side street. "There's a wild bird sanctuary. You want to go?"

"Sure." Birdworld Kuranda. Interesting.

Justus paid their admission, and then they stepped into the most amazing world Arianna had ever seen. Hundreds of the most colorful birds flew all around them under the protective screen dome.

She carried a guide, but she found she was much less interested in identifying the specific varieties of birds, and much more interested in just enjoying them.

As they stepped onto a covered deck, Justus dumped a handful of bird food into her hand from the brown paper lunch sack they'd purchased with their tickets. He poured some into his own hand next, and instantly a stunning yellow bird landed on his outstretched hand.

Arianna pulled her phone from her back pocket to take pictures. She'd taken shots from the bottom of the mountain and the Skyrail too. Justus hadn't been kidding about photos. He never used his own phone to take pictures.

Luckily, no one from her family had texted or called since they'd started this vacation. The fact that her entire family was in Italy was buying her some time. They were busy with their own vacation. She hadn't posted anything on social media either, mainly because she had no clear idea what she wanted them to know about this fling with Justus. On the one hand, she had never been one to keep secrets from her gigantic family. On the other hand, they would never understand why she would go on a vacation with a man she didn't intend to marry.

There was little chance in hell they would buy some story about Arianna and Justus being nothing more than friends, especially not her mother. It sounded absurd even silently in her head. Maybe she would simply ignore any incoming calls or texts. At least until she and Justus had a chat about what her response should be. The clock was ticking, though. She couldn't ignore her family forever. Eventually, someone, probably her mother, would contact her.

It was possible her parents and most of her siblings weren't even aware Justus was in Australia at all. If Tony didn't think twice about hooking her up to help Justus with his travel plans, maybe he didn't mention it to anyone else in the family. Slim chance, but possible.

Considering Tony was in Rome too, he sure wasn't going to call and check up on her.

She jerked her attention back to Justus when he ducked his head as a colorful red-and-blue bird landed on top. His movement did nothing to distract the bird, however, nor did it bother the yellow one for a single second. The yellow one continued to dine on the feast in Justus's hand.

Arianna took a dozen pictures.

Eventually, they extricated themselves from the throng of birds on that deck and wandered through the winding bridge that took them all around the sanctuary. As they rounded the last bend on their way toward the exit, someone spoke. "Arianna?"

She lifted her gaze to find Chris standing two feet in front of her. He beamed and lifted a hand toward Justus. "And Justus, right? We must have had the same travel agent," he joked.

Justus shook his hand, albeit reluctantly, judging by the

pressure of his other hand on Arianna's back. *Great.* Just what they needed. Another encounter. Another disagreement. He did *not* point out that Arianna was in fact their very own travel planner. "Must have."

"Did you guys eat yet?" Chris asked. He pointed toward the exit. "I was just going to grab some lunch. I saw an amazing crêpe restaurant while I was wandering around. I would love the company." He faced them both and cleared his throat. "Or not." He chuckled. "I don't want to intrude."

Arianna smiled. "Sounds delightful. I love crêpes. Please, join us."

Chris turned around and headed for the exit. He was several feet in front of them when Justus mocked her in a low voice. "Yes, please. How delightful."

She swatted his chest and shot him a glare. "Be nice. They guy's fiancée left him at the altar," she hissed.

Justus rolled his eyes.

*Great. Wonderful.*

It was only a short walk to the restaurant that clearly charmed Arianna. She was nearly giddy as they took seats on an outdoor patio at what she referred to as a "quaint, little crêpe place."

Justus rather wished the earth would swallow him whole since he'd prefer to be anywhere on the planet alone with Arianna, while at the same time nowhere in the presence of this Chris character.

Perhaps Justus was being unreasonable due to the fact that his days with Arianna were numbered and he didn't want to share her, but the more time they spent with Chris, the higher the hairs stood up on Justus's arms.

He couldn't shake the feeling that he'd seen the guy

before, though probably the reality was he could easily star in any villain movie ever produced. He just had that vibe about him. Fake. Skeevy.

Arianna obviously didn't get the same feeling. She chatted away with him about his job and his life story. She even made excuses for Justus, inventing a lie that Justus was introverted and not very social. She patted him on the thigh and shot him a wide-eyed glare that Chris couldn't see.

One thing was for sure, Justus needed to keep his thoughts to himself or risk arguing with Arianna for the duration of their trip.

The guy looked normal enough, he supposed. Clean-shaven. Dressed like any other tourist. His clothes were a little worn and shabby, but Justus wouldn't judge a man based on something like that.

The crêpes were delicious. At least there was that bonus. Since every single item on the menu looked amazing to Justus, he'd let Arianna choose, and they shared both a savory and a sweet.

Justus even managed not to roll his eyes dramatically when Chris changed the subject from his work and home to his finances. It was as if he'd honed in on Justus and Arianna, dubbing them as wealthy for some reason, and deciding he could surely suck something out of them.

The thing that most troubled Justus was that he knew Arianna hadn't had many funds of her own before they'd stumbled upon their inadvertent windfall. She'd graduated from college and taken off to work and play for a year. Maybe she had a few thousand dollars, but that was it.

Justus himself did have money saved up from years of not having expenses, but the military wasn't exactly the sort of job people took to get rich. He was an ordinary guy with a few dollars invested for his future.

So, what made Chris decide he could make a buck off a random couple sitting at a hotel bar? Because Justus was now completely convinced Chris's entire motive was to take advantage of Arianna. In fact, Justus made a mental note to have her leave the cash she was carrying around strapped over her shoulder in the hotel safe from now on.

Hell, she should probably leave the entire purse behind. If she wasn't carrying anything but her phone and whatever else she could fit in her pockets, she wouldn't look like a target for a pickpocket.

"Yeah, I probably shouldn't have come on this trip," Chris was saying, when Justus decided to listen. "If I'd known Shelly had taken everything we jointly owned, I would have stayed home. Lord knows where she is now. Probably some beach vacation living off my money."

"I assume you contacted the authorities," Justus stated, joining in only because he hoped to trap Chris in a lie.

Chris shook his head. "Didn't figure it would do any good. Her name was on the account. She technically had a legal right to withdraw it." Of course he hadn't. Justus doubted there even was a woman named Shelly. He doubted Chris had ever been engaged at all. He wasn't even sure the man was from New Zealand at this point.

"You said she maxed out the credit cards too? Did you freeze them?"

Chris stared blankly for a moment. "I should do that."

*Ya think?*

Then Chris's shoulders fell. "Though it hardly matters right now since she can't continue to use something that's reached its limit. Thank God I prepaid for nearly everything on this trip, otherwise I would be stranded. As it is, I'm really only hard up for meals."

*Of course you are. How convenient.*

Arianna reached for the creep and set a hand on his

shoulder. "I'm so sorry. What a mess. I can't even imagine. Lunch is on us." She jerked her hand back, and without glancing at Justus, she opened her damn purse and pulled out two hundred dollars, handing it to Chris. "Here. Take this. At least you can relax, knowing you'll be able to eat for the rest of the vacation."

Justus stiffened, but it was too late to stop her, and besides, he decided maybe it might be perfect that she'd given Chris that money. Maybe the man would leave them alone now. If Justus could have Arianna all to himself without having to share her with a vagrant for the rest of the trip, it would be well worth the two hundred dollars.

Chris held the money, staring at it and then lifting his gaze to Arianna. "I can't take this. It's for your own holiday." He held it out as if he intended to give it back.

Arianna shook her head. "Don't worry about it. We've been fortunate. Just paying it forward."

Justus held his breath. If she mentioned the ring or the reward, he might lose his shit. Luckily, she did not.

Chris wiped the corner of his eye as he quietly mumbled his thanks.

Justus barely managed to avoid groaning at the ridiculously fake display of emotion. Instead, he gritted his teeth and paid their bill. Finally, the meal was over. If only they could shake this creep...

The three of them stood, and thank God Chris excused himself, saying he was going to head back down on the Skyrail. He waved at them as he wandered off, and Justus finally released a long breath.

Arianna faced him, set her hands on his chest, and glared at him. "Stop it. You're being dramatic. He's just a guy down on his luck. Besides, I gave him money. I doubt we'll see him again if that's what he was after."

Justus rubbed his hands up and down her arms and

then leaned in to kiss her forehead. "You're sweet and kind and so very naïve. I hope you're right, but I'd bet my last dollar we haven't seen the last of Chris Metz, or whatever his name is."

She gave Justus a dazzling smile. "Is this a real bet?"

Justus smirked. "Whatcha got to bet with, baby?" he teased.

"Mmm." She bit her lower lip for a moment and then released it to smile. "Sex."

His eyes widened. "Pardon? What are you planning to do? Withhold it if you're right?"

"Nope." She spun around, giggling as she took his hand and dragged him down the path toward the souvenir shops. When they were out of earshot, she stopped, lifted onto her toes, and whispered, "If I win, and we don't see Chris again, you have to take me to a super fancy restaurant all dressed up with several courses and expensive wine before taking me back to the hotel room and ravaging my body until I've come so many times I lose track."

He chuckled. "How is that a loss for me? Hell, we have plenty of money. We can go shopping right now, buy any dress you want, and dine at the finest place in town." He leaned in closer, setting his lips on her ear. "I can't think of anything I'd rather do than spend hours worshipping your body. Be careful what you wish for."

She shivered, and her cheeks were flushed when he leaned back.

"Let's hear it," he said.

"What?"

He laughed again. "The other half of the bet. It was your idea. What do I get when I win?" He lifted a finger. "And passing him in the hotel lobby doesn't count. That's a distinct possibility. The bet only applies if he worms his way into our plans again, joining us at a table or the bar or on an excursion. It has to be a situation where he manages to get us to pay for something."

She nodded. "Agreed."

"Good. So what do I win?"

She winked at him. "A sexy striptease complete with lingerie and heels, followed by me fucking you in whatever position you want."

It was totally not like him, but damn if he didn't blush too. He wrapped an arm around her and yanked her body flush against his. With his lips hovering so close, they brushed hers before he said, "Baby, I don't think you would be much of a loser in that scenario any more than I would be in the other."

But damn he sure would enjoy watching her strip for him. A little music. Some wine. Her tanned skin in a sexy teddy... "Do I get to pick the lingerie?"

"We'll see." She gave him a quick peck on the lips and then spun out of his arms again. "Come on. There's more to see in Kuranda."

# CHAPTER 12

When Arianna opened her eyes the following morning, she found Justus propped on an elbow, staring down at her, grinning. "Ha," he said immediately. "I finally woke up before you. I think I'm acclimated."

She smiled as she rolled toward him, pushing him onto his back and flattening herself to his side. "What time is it?"

He ran a hand up and down her naked back, making her shiver. "Seven. We have to get moving. We're supposed to be at the dock to meet the snorkel tour boat by eight."

"Mmm. How long is the trip? I forgot."

"It's a full day. Aren't you proud? I even looked at your itinerary. We won't be back until tonight. It takes a long time to get to the Great Barrier Reef. They serve us lunch on the boat."

She kissed his chest and then flicked her tongue over his nipple.

He grabbed her shoulders. "We'll be late if you do that." He wiggled out from under her and scooted off the bed, jerking out of her reach when she went after him. His damn fine ass filled her vision as he padded to the bathroom.

She flopped onto her back and smiled up at the ceiling. Best. Vacation. Ever. Nothing would top this in her lifetime. The sexiest man in the world that she'd lusted after since she'd been a young teenager had proven to be even better than her wildest imagination.

How many times had she visualized him kissing her, his hands roaming all over her body, his cock pressing against her? Hundreds. And the reality was even better. She wasn't fourteen anymore. Her imagination had grown over the years. Though she hadn't seen him in a long time, she'd never stopped fantasizing. Recently, she'd added to the fantasies—his mouth pressed against her sex, his cock buried inside her, his hands holding her down…

"What are you grinning about?" he asked, his hands planted next to her, one knee on the bed. She hadn't heard him return.

"I'm just happy." She cupped his face. "Thanks for spending your holiday with me."

"My pleasure. Just you, me, and Chris Metz. Fantasies come true."

She rolled her eyes. "Come on. Be fair. I'm going to win the bet. I promise we won't see him again." Arianna was confident. The guy was too humble to join them again. She'd seen the pain in his eyes. He'd felt horrible accepting their money.

Justus shoved off the bed and then reached across and grabbed Arianna by the waist, hauling her to her feet. "Grab a bikini. Let's get moving."

∾

Justus didn't breathe easily until he was settled on the boat, his arm around Arianna, a couple they hadn't met before sitting across the table from them, and no sign of Chris.

From the moment they'd boarded, he'd started scanning the occupants, keeping a close eye on the dock. It wasn't until the boat pulled away that he finally fully exhaled.

Arianna shot him several glares, but she didn't say a word. She knew him well enough to realize he'd been expecting Chris to show up. She even smirked at him when they left port.

The couple who'd been assigned to share their table was about their age. Friendly. Fun. Also on vacation. Arianna chatted with them from the moment they'd sat down. As soon as Justus could relax, he joined the conversation.

The weather was beautiful. The sun was out. The temperature was not too cold.

Justus loved spending time with Arianna. She was radiant. Her thick hair was down and blowing around, which he suspected she did for him because she knew he liked it.

He spent most of the boat ride sitting cocked to the side next to her, one hand on the back of their bench seat, his fingers toying with her hair as she chatted. Every time she looked his direction, her face was flushed and her eyes danced with warmth.

He was falling for her. Harder than he'd ever thought possible. He hadn't thought he was even capable of such a thing, and it was completely against his personal policy. He needed to find a way to rein in his emotions and keep his heart guarded. Maintaining any sort of relationship with her after this vacation was out of the question.

To the best of his knowledge, she hadn't spoken to anyone in her family since he'd arrived. He'd noticed a text from Tony had come in while they were sleeping, but he'd ignored it. Tony was still oblivious. His text had been brief, asking if Justus had found Arianna okay. Justus and Arianna still needed to bump heads and figure out what sort of story they were going to tell after this trip so their narrative was the same.

Lying to Tony seemed out of the question. Telling Tony that Justus had slept with his sister and then left her high and dry was also out of the question. It was a conundrum he really should have put more thought into before letting his dick run the show.

He shook thoughts of the future from his mind as the boat anchored and then he and Arianna headed for the rear of the ship to get their wetsuits and snorkeling gear. He'd worn many wetsuits in his life. This was Arianna's first time.

He laughed as she jumped up and down, trying to get the suit over her hips and then up her body.

"You gonna help? Or just use me for your personal humor?" She was still grinning as she leaned toward him and kissed him briefly, the suit hanging halfway up her body, her fantastic tits hanging in front of him, clad only in a skimpy white bikini.

He grabbed the suit alongside her hips and jerked it upward, lifting her clear off the ground. It worked, though. The last part of the bottom slid over her ass as she squealed, grabbing his shoulders. "*Justus.*"

"What? You're in." He lifted the back half and helped guide her arms into the sleeves. The suit was tight around her hourglass body. Never before had he considered a wetsuit sexy, but today, even though it was covering up her far sexier string bikini, somehow on Arianna, it made his dick hard.

She awkwardly struggled with the mask and snorkel next, and then the fun part. The fins.

"Baby, don't put them on until you're sitting on the edge of the back of the boat ready to jump in. It's too hard to walk in them, and nearly impossible to navigate the steps down to the water." He took them from her hand and carried both of their pairs to the back of the boat.

It was crowded with everyone aiming to get into the water. Luckily, they had been assigned time slots to cut down on the jam of people and confusion. There was no reason to be in a hurry. They would have more than enough time in the water.

Justus handed Arianna her fins as they sat next to each other, legs dangling inches above the water. He slid his on at the same time as her. "Ready?" he asked as he settled his goggles over his eyes.

"Yep. Can't wait." She shoved off the edge right before him, hitting the water with a splash.

The moment he joined her and put his face in the water, he knew this trip had been well worth it. An entire colorful world of fish awaited them. When he tipped his face toward Arianna under the water, he could see even through her mask that her eyes were wide with excitement.

She grabbed his hand and they swam several yards away from the boat. Every few seconds, she pointed at something.

It was hard not to grin and take water into his mouth while seeing the Great Barrier Reef through the eyes of Arianna. Even though he'd never been to this part of the world, he'd been snorkeling in many places around the globe.

The reef itself was a bit depressing. Most of its color was washed out as it was slowly dying off. The fish were stunning, however. He could float here at sea, soaking in the array of vibrant colors for hours.

It was hard to keep track of another person in the water, but he managed to keep an eye on Arianna and usually had a hand on her body somewhere. Hip. Back. Legs. Arm. Anything. It wasn't entirely necessary, but he found he liked to be near her, keep her close. Even during this excursion that had permitted very little interaction and no conversation, he wanted to connect with her.

She returned the favor, often clasping his hand or settling hers on some part of his body. When they finally returned to the boat, starving for lunch, she was all smiles. "My God, that was beautiful," she said as soon as they popped out of the water and removed their snorkels.

"It was." He pulled her close, though it was hard to maintain contact since they were both bobbing up and down in the water. "Thank you for planning this excursion. Hell, thank you for planning all of them. You've done a fantastic job. But this one was the best."

"My pleasure. Thank *you* for allowing me to come along."

"It wasn't as if you gave me options," he teased. "You hijacked my vacation."

"Are you sorry?" she lifted a brow, grinning.

"Not for a second." He managed a brief kiss in the constantly moving water. "Let's get back on the boat."

Hauling himself up the steps wasn't a problem. Reaching down to take Arianna's hand and get her on board proved comical. But finally they managed to get their fins off, wiggle out of the wetsuits, and return the gear.

Lunch was delicious. The trip back was peaceful.

Arianna even leaned against his chest and napped for a while. He enjoyed every second. After all, it was his turn to watch her sleep, which he'd had the pleasure of twice in one day.

Life was good.

## CHAPTER 13

Even though they hadn't showered and should have been exhausted, Justus suggested they stop for dinner and a few beers along the way back to the hotel. The street that led from the dock to the hotel had a sidewalk that meandered along the water with restaurants lining the other side of the street.

Every bar and pizza joint and burger place had outdoor seating. The air was warm enough to sit outside, so they chose an Italian restaurant, and Justus immediately ordered them both a local beer.

Arianna laughed when she saw him glancing around. She took a sip of the draft beer and set it down. "You're going to lose this bet, Justus."

He shot her a glare. "Doubtful."

"Mmm." She set her elbows on the table and met his gaze.

He did the same. "It was nice having you all to myself today."

"So greedy. *Tsk.* You barely shared me with the fish." But she didn't mind. Not for a second. It was amazing spending time with someone who paid that much attention to her. No man she'd ever dated cared that much.

He did care, right? Was she reading more into it than she should?

She shuddered and looked away. She needed to rein in her emotions before she fell so hard for him that she couldn't salvage her heart. He was leaving in less than a week. He would return to a war zone. She would be here in Australia finishing out her year of work and holiday.

It didn't matter if she was willing to lift her ban on dating military men. He wasn't available to date. Besides, he'd made it clear he had the same policy as her. They were a perfect match for a fling. Except she hadn't expected to enjoy him quite this much.

"Whatcha thinking?" he asked.

She shifted her gaze back to his. "I was trying to remember what time we have to meet the tour guide tomorrow."

"Eight, I think. Same as today. You planned us another long tour."

"This one won't involve water, though." She took another drink of beer. Tonight they were enjoying Two Turtles pale ale. It was smooth and mild and perfect for the evening.

He sighed. "That's too bad. Spending the day with you in that bikini wasn't a hardship."

She chuckled. "It was usually covered up. Not sure it was that interesting." In fact, she had a sundress on over it right now. Also white.

His hand landed on her knee under the table. "Yeah, but knowing it's there is enough to make me forgo dinner and rush you back to the room." His hand slid up her thigh, precariously close to her pussy, before he pulled it away. The action left her mouth dry and her sex wet.

She swallowed. "Do you have any idea what you do to me?" Her voice was husky, unrecognizable. And she squirmed in her seat, squeezing her legs together.

"Yep. That's why I do it." He leaned back, sipping his beer. Cool as a cucumber. At least outwardly. She'd love the opportunity to set her hand on his cock and see how hard it was.

She put her elbows on the table and decided to flat-out ask. "Are you hard for me?"

He nearly choked on his beer and then set the glass on the table, his hand shaking. "Always."

"But right now. More than usual?" she pressed.

"Yes." He reached across the table and took both her hands in his, rubbing his thumbs over her skin. "You're a gorgeous woman, inside and out. I was hard for you the moment I first set eyes on you in Sydney."

She giggled. "You didn't even know who I was."

He lifted a brow, as if to say, *And?*

She giggled again, loving that she had this effect on him. This banter in public was fun. "I have you beat then."

"Pardon? I saw you first. You were looking down at your computer screen, unaware of my approach."

She lifted both brows, tipping her head to one side. "But I've fantasized about you for almost a decade. You didn't know I existed."

He squeezed her hands. "True. You've got me there. And it's a good thing. It would have been extremely creepy and borderline illegal for me to have noticed you at fourteen."

"Man, did I work hard to get you to notice me back then. I knew I was too young. I knew you were leaving for the navy. But I worked it. You have no idea."

He rubbed her hands again, his expression serious. "I'm sorry I didn't pay attention. That must have been hurtful."

She shook her head. "It was a girl's dream. I wasn't mad. It was more of a challenge. I knew I was gangly. A late bloomer. I had crazy, curly hair that stuck out in every direction. My boobs were flat. I hadn't even started my period."

"Let's not get carried away. You were cute. It's not as if I don't remember you existing. But you were Tony's little sister. You had a pretty smile. I knew you were book smart. I knew you had an amazing future ahead of you."

"Thank you," she murmured. He had no idea how his kind words affected her. Just knowing he'd even noticed her for a moment was something.

He wiggled his eyebrows. "Tell me what you did to get me to notice you."

Her face heated and she rolled her eyes. "Now?"

"Yes. I want to hear it." He leaned closer, tucking a lock of hair behind her ear. "I want to know what kind of crush fourteen-year-old Arianna had on an older guy like me."

She licked her lips. "Mmm. Well, for one thing, I experimented with makeup one time when you were over. My parents weren't home, so I tried eyeshadow and mascara. Unfortunately, I accidentally scratched my eye with the mascara wand, and the blue lines of eyeshadow made me look like a clown. When Tony spotted me, he lifted both brows. I ran from the room before you noticed, mortified."

Justus laughed. "Sorry I missed that."

She smiled, remembering another incident. "Then there was the time I borrowed my friend's jean skirt, but I was much taller than her, so it wasn't long enough. Not only did it barely cover my butt, but I looked like a porn star. Luckily, you didn't notice that time either." She leaned her chin on her palm. "I was both disappointed and relieved.

Tony wasn't pleased with my antics that time either, but I don't think he realized I had a crush on you."

"Speaking of Tony, he's going to kill me." Justus sighed, releasing her hands and taking another swig of beer.

"Not if we don't tell him."

Justus met her gaze. "I've considered that, but I can't wrap my head around it. He's going to ask me a dozen questions because that's the kind of guy he is. 'How was your trip? Did Arianna plan it well? Is Arianna doing well? Did she seem safe? Does she have a boyfriend? Did you see much of her?' In fact, he texted me during the night. I haven't responded."

Arianna blew out a breath. "You're right. And worse than that, everyone in my family is going to ask me questions about you. My parents have always adored you. I'll get the third degree when they find out I went on a vacation with you. It's shocking that no one has reached out to me yet. I'm sure at least my mother is going to check in with me soon. Even though they are in Rome, they don't usually go very many days without making contact."

Justus nodded. "Yeah, we're kinda fucked. We definitely need a united plan."

"We met up. I had some time. I went with you to show you the sights." She sat straighter. That would work, right?

"Uh-huh." Justus smirked. "The first thing out of Tony's mouth is going to be, 'Did you fuck my sister?'"

She cringed. "Well, we have a week to figure it out. You better at least answer Tony before he starts to worry."

Justus nodded and pulled out his phone, typing up a quick text and then showing it to her.

*Arianna is doing great. She planned my entire trip. Hope Rome is amazing.*

"That'll work," she stated.

He hit send, groaning. "I hate lying to your brother, even if it is by omission."

As soon as they were back in the hotel room, Justus had his hands on Arianna's body. The second after she set her purse down and kicked off her sandals, he grabbed the hem of her dress and tugged it over her head.

Goose bumps rose on her skin as he held her at arm's length and let his gaze roam up and down her sexy body. The white string bikini was indeed fucking hot against her darker skin. She'd put a band in her hair when they went snorkeling, and it was still there, so he reached to pull it free. Thick curls fell around her shoulders.

When his gaze reached her eyes, he found her already breathless. He'd seen the pucker of her nipples under the white triangles. He thought he could even smell her arousal soaking her skimpy bottoms.

He slid his hands up from her hips to cup her breasts, making her gasp. As he took her lips, he marveled at how responsive she was to him. Every day. Even if they had sex three times, she was always equally aroused. Hot for him. As he was for her.

Was she like that with everyone she slept with, or was it him? If her reaction was strictly for him, they were in a heap of trouble. Because he was more aware every day that if he ever wanted to have a relationship with a woman, Arianna would be his perfect partner.

*But you don't need or want a woman in your life*, he reminded himself as he angled the kiss to take it deeper.

Arianna moaned into his mouth, her hands fisting his shirt. He loved the way she got so lost in his kisses that she couldn't get her limbs to respond to commands. Her jerky movements told him she would love to yank his shirt off, if only her fingers were receiving messages from her brain.

Finally, he released her lips and pulled his shirt over his head for her.

She flattened her palms on his chest and smoothed them up to cup his neck and the back of his head. "Your body is a work of art," she murmured. "Your skin is so smooth." Her hands ran up and down his back now as she murmured against his lips. "And these muscles…" Her fingers slid to his chest, molding over his pecs. "There isn't an ounce of fat on you."

He cupped the backs of her thighs and then lifted her off the floor. "Wrap your legs around me."

She did so immediately.

He backed her up toward the desk and set her ass on the surface.

She remained tight around him, her ankles clasped at his lower back.

He resumed kissing her, wishing his swim trunks and the light track pants he'd covered them with would somehow disappear on their own. When that didn't work, he released her neck, tucked his hands under her thighs, and tugged both articles of clothing over his hips.

He shimmied his body enough to make the material fall to the floor, leaving him naked. Now he just needed to divest her of the bikini, which wouldn't be hard since it was literally tied in several places at her back and hips.

Nibbling a path to her shoulder, he tugged the ties at her neck and back first, and then as the bikini fell away, he grabbed the strings at both hips simultaneously. Seconds later, she was as naked as him.

She gasped and tightened her legs around his waist when his length rubbed against her opening. Warm. Wet.

Needy. "Please," she murmured, writhing her hips against him.

Her movements were more than he could take, so he lined himself up with her pussy and thrust into her.

Arianna cried out, her head falling back.

He didn't move, waiting for her to focus, not wanting to come too fast. Not wanting this moment to end.

But she squirmed, her breasts bouncing, her fingers digging into his shoulders. When she met his gaze, her eyes were glazed. "Move," she croaked out.

He couldn't deny her. Not another moment. So he pulled out and thrust back in. Damn. It felt so good. Better than any other time he'd fucked her. Something about the angle or the fact that they'd gone all day without having sex. Something about the way her skin was darker from a day in the sun or the way her nipples puckered.

He tried to focus his attention on the two swollen globes, flicking his thumbs over the tips.

"Justus..." she demanded.

He didn't want to come yet, so he set his attention on her instead, sliding one set of fingers down between their bodies to find her clit hot and swollen. He rubbed her there, watching her face as her mouth fell open. Seconds later, she stiffened and gasped as she came. Damn. She was so fucking amazing.

Before she came down, while her body was still pulsing around him, he grabbed her hips again and pulled almost out before thrusting back in. Again. And again. So fucking good. Too good.

He lowered his gaze just as he was about to come, wanting to watch himself thrusting into her. Just as he was about to lose control, he realized why she felt too damn fantastic.

On a long groan, he jerked out of her, wrapped his

hand around his length, and pumped his fist for the two seconds it took to finish himself off. His orgasm came fast, long stripes of his come landing on her thighs and belly.

He was half-aware of her also watching, both their heads tipped down between their bodies. When he was finally spent, he released his dick and closed his eyes, fighting for a deep breath. "God, Arianna, I'm so sorry."

"For what?" she whispered, her hands running up and down his back. "That was the sexiest thing I've ever seen."

He groaned again and then opened his eyes. "I forgot the condom. That was inexcusable."

She squeezed his shoulder blades. "It's okay. I'm on birth control."

He wrapped his arms around her, pulled her body flush against his, and gently tucked a loose strand of hair behind her ear. He didn't give a shit that his come was smeared between them. "I swear I've never had sex without a condom before. I got so caught up that I didn't even realize why it felt so much better than ever before. I thought it was just you."

She smiled broadly. "Maybe it *was* me."

He closed his eyes, his hand reached into the hair at the back of her head to pull her face against his chest.

*Maybe she's right. Maybe it's her. I'm so screwed.*

# CHAPTER 14

"I'm beginning to think you two are stalking me." The grating voice followed by an equally annoying chuckle made Justus lift his gaze to find exactly the man he expected. Chris Metz. Great. Another day of vacation brought to a screeching halt.

They were on the tour bus, already seated, when Chris magically joined them. It was as if the man had a copy of their fucking itinerary and plotted each stop.

Arianna's fingers dug into Justus's thigh where her hand rested. She didn't need to speak out loud for him to hear her words. *Be nice.* She smiled at Chris as he took a seat across the aisle next to her. Of course. "Hey. We missed you yesterday at the Great Barrier Reef," she joked.

He cringed. "I don't do boats. Sea sickness."

"Bummer. It was amazing."

Chris leaned forward to make eye contact with Justus. "Can't thank you enough for helping me out."

Justus nodded. "No worries. Glad we could help." There was no sense in being antagonistic. He had no proof the man was an asshole. Everything about him screamed fraud, but Justus couldn't very well raise a stink over a gut feeling. Besides, he would do anything to keep the peace with Arianna. No way was he going to let this Chris character mess up Justus's evenings.

When Chris turned to speak to the other person sharing his bench seat, Justus blew out a long breath and leaned close to Arianna's ear. He set his hand high on her thigh and ran it up under her skirt. "What color is that lingerie going to be?"

She giggled and turned toward him, her hand landing on his and squeezing to keep him from straying higher. "I don't think this counts yet. So far it's more like an accidental encounter," she whispered.

Justus lifted both brows and smirked. "Fine. Okay." In a way she was right. Until Chris invited himself to join their plans and convinced them to pay for something, he wouldn't choose the color of Arianna's teddy, but he would let himself visualize her strutting around the hotel room wearing it. His cock got hard at the thought.

Maybe this day wouldn't be a total bust. After all, he felt confident by the end of the day he would be leaning back on the love seat in the hotel room while the sexiest woman he knew danced for him.

She narrowed her gaze, eyeing him suspiciously, as he adjusted his dick.

He shrugged. "Just visualizing my evening."

She flushed, but the slightest giggle escaped. All was not lost.

Luckily, Justus didn't have to engage with Chris on the bus ride. He did, however, keep one hand dangled over Arianna's shoulder, toying with the spaghetti strap of her sun dress while she chatted with Chris. If the man had any thoughts of stealing Justus's woman, he was sadly mistaken.

In fact, Justus decided then and there to take the high road. Instead of running the risk of angering the woman he intended to be inside that night, he would dig deep and find a way to behave in the fakest manner imaginable.

When the bus pulled up to their first stop, the Wildlife Habitat, Chris exited the bus chatting it up with whoever had shared his seat. Apparently that person was also traveling alone.

Justus was relieved. He kept a very slow pace for the first part of the stop, pretending to be overly interested in each animal and encouraging Arianna to take several pictures. If she caught on to his diversion, she said nothing.

It wasn't a hardship since this particular zoo was very cool. The animals were roaming free in many of their natural habitats, even walking right up to the guests. He took several pictures of Arianna posing with kangaroos, wallabies, cassowaries, birds, crocodiles, and koalas.

"This is the place where we get to have our picture taken holding a koala," Arianna exclaimed as she took his hand and lured him toward the photo station.

Out of all the things they'd seen and done so far on this magical vacation, Justus had to admit, holding a koala topped his list. The little guys were damn cute, though their claws were shockingly sharp against his chest, and they smelled strongly of eucalyptus.

The time went by too quickly, and two hours later they were back on the bus heading for Mossman Gorge. Once again, Justus had to endure a rambling conversation between Arianna and Chris while they rode to the next stop, but he tuned it out, closing his eyes and feigning a nap.

He kept his hand draped around Arianna's shoulders again, and she didn't balk but held his fingers where they dangled in front of her breast. Just to torment her, he let the tips of his fingers brush across her nipple every once in a while.

She squirmed with each contact, causing him to smile, but he didn't open his eyes to meet her gaze each time he sensed her angling her face toward him.

The irony in this entire ongoing saga was that Arianna had convinced Chris that Justus was introverted and quiet. Nothing could be farther from the truth, but at least she provided him with an excuse not to engage the man.

At the next stop, the group from the bus hiked a short distance to the gorge. The view was spectacular from deep inside the Daintree Rainforest.

Chris stayed on their heels during the hike, but the fact that their tour guide was speaking about the local flora most of the time kept him from yapping away at Arianna.

"Would you like me to take a picture of the two of you together?" Chris asked when they reached the gorge. Oh yeah, Justus was so totally going to win this bet with Arianna. No way could she deny that Chris was stuck to them like white on rice. All that was left was for Chris to con them into paying for something. It was only a matter of time.

"That would be great. Thank you so much." Arianna handed him her phone.

Justus wrapped both arms around Arianna from behind and held her back flush against his chest for the picture. As Chris handed Arianna's phone back, Justus considered the fact that most of their photos from the trip consisted of selfies. If Arianna intended to document the vacation in any way or show family members a slideshow of this side trip during her year abroad, she wouldn't be able to avoid the dozens of pictures that clearly demonstrated she was Justus's temporary significant other. He wasn't simply in nearly every picture; he had his arms wrapped around her as if they were married in most of them.

He took her phone from her before she could slide it back in her pocket.

"What?" she asked.

"Let me take a few of you alone in front of the gorge."

"Okaaayyy," she drawled out. "Why?"

He took several shots and gave her the phone back.

"What was that all about?"

He took her hand in his as they headed back down the path. "Thought you might want some shots with just you in them."

Arianna said nothing in response until they were back on the bus and seated. She turned her body to face Justus. Her face was serious. "I don't think I can lie about this trip, Justus."

He stared at her a moment and then sighed. "I hear you. I'm not sure I can either." It seemed impossible. "We probably need to discuss our game plan soon." He pulled her closer and kissed her gently at the moment Chris boarded and took his seat across the aisle. It was intentional.

Justus didn't really think Chris was interested in Arianna romantically. He truly believed the man was a swindler. But just in case...

She rolled her eyes when the kiss ended. "You did that on purpose," she whispered.

"Yep." He gave her a cocky grin and sat back, holding her hand against his thigh to keep her close.

After stopping for lunch, the bus took off once more for their final stop, a pontoon trip along the shore of the Daintree River. The bus let them off and continued to the other side of the river by the ferry where it would pick them back up after the tour.

The afternoon sun was warm as Justus led Arianna to a seat near the front of the pontoon. He was relieved when Chris picked another spot on the boat, and soon they were pulling away from the shore. The guide was hilarious and filled with information about the mangroves and crocodiles. He paused the pontoon several times to point out crocodiles along the shore. Young and old. Small and incredibly large.

"I think I've had my fill of crocodiles for a lifetime," Arianna declared on the return trip. She shuddered. "They give me the willies."

"They should," Justus pointed out. "The darn things are vicious. I'd rather not die by drowning because a crocodile held me underwater."

Chris chimed in from across the aisle again, of course. "Sounds like you'll be fine as long as you always respect their habitat and keep your distance."

"It's amazing how many people ignore the warnings," Arianna added. She leaned her head against Justus's shoulder and closed her eyes. In moments, she was asleep.

Justus was grateful. For one, he loved watching her sleep. For another, her nap kept Chris from talking nonstop. Justus didn't give the man any vibe that insinuated he was willing to engage. Besides, there would be no way to avoid disturbing Arianna if they spoke over her.

Justus didn't get the feeling Chris had nearly as much interest in Justus as he did Arianna, anyway, which wasn't hard to believe considering Arianna had presented herself as incredibly kind and outgoing while Justus had spent nearly every moment in Chris's company scowling.

When the bus finally pulled up in front of their hotel, Justus was still trying to decide which of them had won the bet. Their encounter with Chris had seemingly been accidental, so Arianna could argue that she won. However, Justus wasn't willing to consent yet. There was still plenty of time for Chris to worm his way into their evening and score something financial.

As soon as they stepped into the lobby, Justus was proven right.

"Would you two like to join me for dinner? It's on me. I feel bad about taking your money the other day. I have most of it still in my pocket."

Before Justus could turn down the offer, Arianna beat him to it. "Thanks, but I'm exhausted. Even after that long nap, I still feel like I could sleep for ten hours. I think we're going to call it an early night."

Chris nodded. "No worries. You two enjoy yourselves."

Justus held back a fist pump as he led Arianna through the lobby and into the elevator.

"Stop gloating," she said as the doors slid shut. She swatted his chest. "I think that was a draw. We didn't pay for anything, and the encounter was accidental."

Justus turned toward her and stalked into her space until he had her pressed against the wall of the elevator. He cupped her face while he flattened his front against hers. "I don't care who wins or loses the bet. I figure I win either way. What I do care about is that you turned down dinner with him, and now I get you all to myself in the room for the rest of the night."

The door slid open before he had a chance to kiss her, but she was smiling as he snagged her hand and dragged her quickly down the hallway to their room.

As soon as they were inside, he grabbed her waist, making her squeal as he once again flattened her to the door. This time he kissed her thoroughly, not coming up for air until she moaned. "God, I love that sound."

"For the record, there wasn't a chance in hell I was

going to agree to dine with Chris or anyone else on the planet. We only have a few days left together. I'm not sharing them with anyone."

Justus slid his hands up her torso and then around to cup her breasts. "Good. You won't get an argument out of me on that subject. But I do think you need to start thinking about what color teddy you intend to buy," he teased. He intentionally flicked his thumbs over her breasts as he spoke.

As expected, Arianna drew in a sharp breath and rose onto her toes. He was beginning to anticipate her every response, and he liked it. What did it say about them that the sex hadn't even begun to get old? It was probably too early to make that sort of leap, but they definitely had more chemistry than the average couple.

What he didn't know was what the hell he was going to do about it or how it was going to affect their future. The thought of walking away from Arianna and never looking back made his chest hurt.

The thought of not walking away from her seemed impossible and unimaginable.

# CHAPTER 15

Arianna woke up the next morning to find Justus staring down at her yet again. She smiled. "I guess my days of watching you sleep are over."

"Yep." He brushed a lock of hair from her face and pulled her more fully under him. "I noticed you marked today as a lazy day on our itinerary."

"I did." She ran her hand up his chest. "What do you want to do with all this extra time I blocked in?"

"I think shopping and then an amazing dinner."

His words shocked her. "Shopping? I didn't peg you for a shopping guy. Like souvenirs?"

He grinned. "Nope. I mean, I made reservations for dinner. You're gonna need a dress, and I need a tie."

She opened her eyes wider. "I thought we determined neither of us really won that bet."

He shrugged. "Doesn't matter. I still want to take you to dinner." He trailed a finger down her cheek and then her neck and around her breast.

It was amazing how her body responded to him no matter how many times they had sex. First thing in the morning, halfway through the day, later in the evening. She was constantly turned on by his touch.

From the moment they'd stepped over the line and turned this into an intimate relationship, he'd been touching her. In fact, there had been very few instances when they'd been separated for more than minutes. Pretty much only when one of them was in the bathroom. They'd even shared showers most days.

Arianna stared into his eyes, a sudden sadness making her swallow back the lump of emotion welling in her throat. Had this entire plan been a horrible mistake? Why the hell did she think she could vacation with the man she'd had a crush on for years and flush him out of her system?

The entire concept was preposterous. This was Justus Kirkland. Her brother's best friend. A man who'd been to her house hundreds of times while she'd been too young for him to notice her. A man who was considered a part of her extended family by her parents and siblings.

She was in over her head. She was falling hard for him.

No. She'd already fallen. For a man she knew she had no future with. He was going to leave her here in a few days and travel to the other side of the earth to fight more bad guys.

She was going to remain in Australia for two more months and then return to New York to find a grown-up job. Navy SEALs were off limits for long-term relationships. They broke hearts and caused tears.

Besides, he'd made it perfectly clear that he never intended to settle down with a woman. He was married to his job. He was in it for the long haul. He was a career military man. Not husband material. Not even boyfriend material.

This relationship that wasn't even a relationship was

finite. Its expiration date was creeping closer. And her chest seized at the idea.

Justus furrowed his brow. "You okay?"

She swallowed again and cleared her throat. "Yes." She forced a smile. "I like this dinner plan. Let's go shopping."

For several seconds he held her gaze, clearly not buying her lie. He was a smart guy, though. He undoubtedly understood perfectly well what she might be thinking and wisely chose to leave it alone.

After all, it wasn't as if he wasn't into her too. There was no way in hell he could hide his feelings for her. He was attentive to the point of smothering. Lucky for him, she didn't mind his attention one bit. But it spoke volumes. They had a problem, and neither of them was willing to admit it out loud yet.

∽

It turned out Arianna wasn't the kind of woman who needed to go to seven stores and try on dozens of dresses. As soon as they stepped into the first store, she grabbed about four dresses off the racks and headed to the fitting room.

He'd also expected her to model for him or something. Instead, she emerged about five minutes later and breezed right by him. "Meet me outside," she ordered.

Confused, he stepped onto the sidewalk and waited. When she joined him, she had a solid white plastic garment bag around something he could not see. The hanger was draped over her arm. "Ready," she beamed.

He frowned. "Just like that?"

"Just like what? You told me to get a dress. I did. Now, I'm going to need shoes." She headed down the sidewalk at a clipped pace.

He chuckled as he jogged to keep up. "Do I get to see this dress you bought?"

"Yep. Tonight. When we're leaving for dinner."

He laughed. "How mysterious."

She winked at him. "I like to keep you guessing." She stopped walking and nodded her head toward another store. "You go in here and get what you need. I'll go across the street and grab shoes."

So efficient. "Okay. You want me to carry that for you?" he asked, reaching for the dress.

She apparently found that hilarious. "Not a chance in hell," she snickered as she left him standing there in awe.

*Imagine that. A woman who can knock out shopping in less than ten minutes and somehow manage to keep my dick hard while doing so.* He watched her enter the store across the street and then shook his head as he entered the one she'd directed him to.

Black slacks. A new white shirt. Socks. Loafers. A black tie. By the time he had everything and stepped back outside, she was leaning against the window with another bag in her hand that clearly held a shoebox. "Took you long enough," she teased.

He held even more packages than her now, but that didn't stop him from spinning on her and backing her into the display window. On the sidewalk, in the middle of the day, on a busy street filled with pedestrians, he kissed her. Passionately. Holding nothing back. She made him that hot.

When he finally released her lips, her eyes were glazed, and she was struggling to breathe. "Do you have any idea how sexy you are?"

"I'm starting to catch on," she murmured, licking her lips.

He gave her a slow, seductive smile, a plan forming in

his mind to keep her on the edge of her seat for the rest of the day. Aroused. Needy. Craving him. He wouldn't give her more than the occasional kiss. Not until after dinner. He would seduce her until her mind was spinning through several long courses and a bottle of wine.

"Let's go drop all this off at the hotel and then find some lunch," he suggested.

She nodded, still visibly reeling from the kiss. Good.

Justus gently took her dress from her arm and added it to his own garment bag, and then he took her free hand and led her back to the hotel. Instead of entering through the front door and walking through the lobby, he led her to a side door, used his keycard to open it, and then snuck her to a rear elevator.

"Why are we coming in through the back?" she asked as soon as the elevator closed.

He grinned at her. "Because I don't want anything to ruin our day." By anything, he meant a run-in with the ever-present Chris. Even though the man hadn't weaseled his way into their day yet, Justus wouldn't put it past him to follow them around and insert himself in their plans.

Arianna rolled her eyes, but she was smirking. "Are all SEALs as suspicious of people as you are?"

"Most. Yes." He held the elevator door for her as she exited and followed her down the hallway. As soon as he had her inside, he hung their new clothes up in the closet, leaving them in the garment bags, and then grabbed her by the waist to torment her some more.

Her lips were so sweet, the faint taste of blueberry from her earlier muffin lingering. He held her waist again, his thumbs grazing under her breasts because he knew that drove her mad.

As soon as she moaned and rose onto her toes, he released her lips. "Let's go. I'm starving. I saw a cute

Mexican place we could try for lunch." He tugged her back into the hallway before she would protest, and one minute later he had her back in the same elevator.

She wasn't even steady on her feet. He tried hard not to smile too broadly. Instead, he cupped her face and kissed her again.

When the doors opened, he broke the lip lock and led her into the short hallway to the side entrance and back onto the street. "Hungry?" he asked.

"My head is spinning, actually. What's the rush?" She grabbed his arm as they walked, wrapping her fingers around his elbow and pulling up close to his body.

He glanced down at her, schooling his face. "No rush." He slowed his pace, as if that were the "rush" in question.

Two blocks to the right, he entered a quaint Mexican restaurant, but not without glancing in every direction and then twisting his neck to ensure Chris was not following them or already eating in this particular establishment. Convinced they'd avoided the leech again, he let the waitress seat them at a booth.

Arianna slid into one side, but Justus joined her on the same side, scooching her over with his hip.

She shook her head, tipping her gaze up to look at him. "You're up to something."

"What?" he asked in mock exaggeration, putting a hand over his chest. "Just because I want to sit next to you?" He lowered his hand to her thigh as he spoke, glad once again she'd worn a short, accessible dress.

She jumped in her seat and gasped when he slid his hand under the hem of her skirt and let his pinky drag along the edge of her panties.

Arianna dropped both of her hands to his and gripped hard. Her face was red, lips parted, pupils dilated. And best of all, her breathing was labored. What she didn't do was glance around. "Justus," she breathed out heavily.

He lifted a brow and moved his pinky right over the wet silk of her panties.

"You've had me on edge for like an hour. If you don't stop teasing, I'm going to come right here on this bench and everyone in the restaurant is going to know," she warned, still breathy.

He flicked his pinky over her covered clit next, and then eased his hand away when she whimpered.

God, he loved how he affected her. It made his pulse pick up and his cock harder than a rock. But it was worth it to watch her expression as he drove her mad.

He left his hand on her thigh, but opened the menu just in time for the waiter to arrive. "Can I interest you in one of our margaritas?"

Justus glanced at Arianna. "Yeah?"

She nodded.

"If you'd like to share, we have a house specialty that serves two."

"Perfect," Justus responded.

As the waiter walked away, Arianna gave his hand a useless shove. "I'll never be able to eat with you torturing me."

He leaned over and kissed her neck. "But it will be so fun watching you squirm."

"Is this Tease Arianna Day or something?"

"Or something." He kissed her neck again because he liked the way she shivered.

She peeled his fingers off her thigh and pressed her legs together, and then she pointed at the menu. "Order us something we can share."

"Done." He set his hand back on her thigh.

She groaned, locking her knees tighter.

"I'll be good. Ish."

She cocked her head to one side and rolled her eyes. "You're up to something."

"Me? Never." He was playing with fire was what he was doing. Why the hell had he gotten up this morning with a plot to make her want him so badly?

*Because you enjoy seeing the desire on her face. Because you like knowing it's for you. Because every moment with her is precious.*

When the margarita came, he ordered. A half an hour later, they were both stuffed and Arianna's cheeks were pink from the tequila. She leaned into him. "I'm gonna need a nap."

"We can make that happen." He paid the bill and then scooted from the booth, wondering how the hell he was going to manage to return to the hotel room with her and keep his cock in his pants. Because that was his intention.

He had no idea why he'd concocted this plan, but he fully intended to see it through. It was worth it. Teasing her and denying her had the desired effect of making her face flush, her lips swollen from nibbling on them, and her eyes glazed. Sexy. So fucking sexy.

Because it was for him.

# CHAPTER 16

Arianna was a hot mess by the time she shut the door to the bathroom later that afternoon, sequestering herself from Justus just long enough to primp and get dressed.

Their "nap" had turned into a make-out session to rival all previous make-out sessions on the face of the earth. Justus had flattened her on her back, leaving her in her dress, and lined his body up with hers. He held both her hands over her head in one of his and kissed her until she writhed against him. He trailed one hand up and down her body, tormenting her breasts and thighs, but rarely hitting the mark.

She moaned and squirmed and eventually begged, but he never left second base and he never let her get off. Eventually, he did let her nap, though it took her fifteen minutes just to catch her breath and keep her mind from focusing on her swollen nipples and clit.

Now, she was locked in the bathroom. She had dried her hair straight and curled the ends under just enough for the thick locks to lay in some semblance of control. She applied more makeup than she had on any day since the first morning when he'd arrived.

Lastly, the dress. It was cream-colored and silky. It hugged her body to perfection. It also didn't permit any undergarments. The back was bare, a swoop of material that left her exposed nearly to her butt. The front neckline plunged, leaving her breasts free under the loose material. The hem reached mid-thigh, but any sort of panties or even a thong would have been obvious.

Cream-colored, strappy heels rounded out the outfit, and then she stared at herself in the mirror for several moments, taking deep breaths. The entire outfit cost more than anything she'd purchased in her life, but with the money they'd received, they'd adapted a mutual fuck-it attitude for the duration of the vacation. Perhaps it was careless, but she couldn't bring herself to deny them this fun.

This trip was already filled with memories that would have to last a lifetime. She intended to add to those in the coming days. If she was truly never going to see Justus again, she wanted to make every second count.

The thought of never seeing him again made her cringe for two reasons. One, it would kill her. Two, it wasn't reasonable to expect. Instead, she would see him occasionally in the future. He was her brother's best friend. He came to the house with Tony when they were on leave. The fact that they hadn't crossed paths while she'd been in college was a fluke. Ordinarily he showed up during holidays.

Would they agree to end this with a clean break in a few days and then spend the rest of their lives pretending it never happened? Could they? Could she?

"Arianna?"

She inhaled slowly and let it out just as slowly, shaking

the painful thoughts away. Finally, she turned and opened the door.

Justus stood there looking like a million bucks. His shirt was starched and crisp. His black slacks hugged his hips perfectly. His tie was centered. And his face. Oh man. His gaze was on her, his mouth hanging open. He gripped the frame of the doorway and rocked in her direction.

His gaze wandered up and down her body again, landing on her face. "Fuck me," he whispered. "I can't take you to dinner wearing that. I won't be able to keep my hands off you."

She smiled. "That's your fault. You could have eased some of the sexual tension at any point during the day. You're the one who denied us both the relief. Now you're stuck." She took a step forward, flattened a palm on his chest, and patted him condescendingly. "Backfire on you, big guy?"

"Apparently," he murmured as he wrapped his fingers around hers and lifted the tips to his lips. He kissed each one and then took a deep breath. "Dinner."

"I'm ready."

Justus was a fool. He should have known she would knock his socks off with whatever mystery dress she'd purchased. As soon as she passed him to step into the hall, his cock doubled in size. Her back was bare. Her gorgeous hair swayed across her naked skin, making his mouth water.

The hem of her dress was just loose enough to swish with every step, but he was fairly certain she wore nothing under the dress.

*Fuck me.*

Without thinking, he led her down the main elevator

and through the lobby. His gaze was only on her as he guided her across the carpet. With the heels, her legs enticed him to lick a line up from her ankles to her pussy. He visualized flattening her on her back, stripped of everything but those heels. He didn't even care if she dug them into his ass.

A low whistle caught his attention, and he jerked his gaze forward to find Chris strolling their direction. "Damn, you two look nice. Going out?"

"Yep." *Obviously*, Justus didn't add. *And alone*, he also refrained from stating.

"Celebrating an anniversary or milestone?" he inquired. His hands were tucked in his jeans, and he was rocking back and forth on the balls of his feet.

"Nope. Just going to dinner." Justus kept her moving forward.

"How much longer will you be in Cairns?" he asked.

It took great strength for Justus to answer him without taking a swing. He seethed at the audacity of the man interrupting his perfect evening. Couldn't he see that now wasn't a good time to chat? Never was also a good time.

Arianna answered. "We aren't sure yet. We haven't decided," she lied, making Justus want to kiss her. The truth was they had a flight out the following afternoon, but Justus would prefer not giving Chris the specifics. With their luck, the man would show up at their next hotel.

"Well, have a nice night." Chris smiled, the expression almost believable.

Justus ushered Arianna out the front door and into a cab. He didn't exhale until he glanced back and found no sign of Chris.

"He really gets under your skin," Arianna commented, her hand on Justus's thigh. She rubbed it up and down, reaching closer to his crotch with every stroke, distracting him.

He twisted his face back to hers and grabbed her hand. With a cocky grin, he shook his head. "That's *my* game," he said as he removed her fingers.

She gave him a fake pout, her face scrunching up. "Why are you the only one who gets to tease?"

"Because I'm bigger and stronger, and this is *my* night." He hated to mess up her lip gloss, but there was no way to put it off another moment, so he smoothed his hand up her bare back under her hair, cupped her neck, and closed the distance for a gentle kiss.

She was panting from the brief contact. "You're going to drive me insane tonight, aren't you?"

"That's the plan."

She didn't look too upset, though. In fact, her eyes twinkled with excitement. "Bring it on."

Arianna was somewhat relieved when she found out they would be seated at a regular table with two chairs on opposite sides. At least Justus wouldn't be able to spend the meal with one hand on her thigh.

Her legs were wobbly and her heart rate elevated from the car ride. As she sat, she crossed one leg over the other, squeezing her thighs together. She was so wet that without any barrier between her pussy and the silk of her dress, she was worried about leaving a wet spot.

Justus ordered a bottle of wine and then stared at her. He looked so serene. Peaceful. Content. Exactly how she felt. She was glad she could confidently assume Chris would not show up in this fancy restaurant since he was obviously short on funds.

She didn't know why Justus found the man so frustrating, but she also didn't want anything to come between them tonight. She needed to trust his instincts. He was a SEAL. She was a civilian. What did she know about reading people?

Assuming nothing was going to happen on that front to mess with their evening, they still had another problem that needed addressing. Now was as good a time as any. If she put it off much longer, she was going to find herself in a bind. "No one has contacted me from my family."

"I noticed that," he responded as he took one of her hands in his. "I assume that concerns you."

"Yes. Not because I think something's wrong, but because I suspect Tony told them I'm with you. The only reason no one would check up on me is if they thought someone else was already doing so."

He leaned forward. "Me."

"Yes."

He sighed and glanced down at their combined hands. It was distracting the way he rubbed his thumb absentmindedly over her knuckles. "You want me to reach out to Tony?"

She winced. "Not really."

He lifted his gaze. "Listen. This is my fault. I wasn't thinking about the bind I was putting you in when we started this adventure. I should have been more considerate of your situation. I'll do whatever you want to make it easier for you."

She nodded, a little choked up and unsure how to respond.

He held her gaze. "Whatever story you want to tell, I'll go along."

"I can't ask you to lie to my brother."

"I didn't say it would be easy, but frankly I'm not

sleeping with your brother, so my allegiance belongs to you on this topic."

She searched his gaze, but it was unwavering. He was dead serious. He would do whatever she wanted. The problem was she didn't know what she wanted, and no scenario seemed acceptable. The only way she could look anyone in the eye and tell them the truth would be if she and Justus hadn't agreed to end things this week.

How the hell were her siblings and parents going to understand a decision she made to spend her vacation sleeping with a man whom she had no intention of seeing again? And what would they think of Justus's role in this? They would be furious with him. She knew it. A man they'd worshipped for years.

"Help me out here. I don't have the answers."

His voice dropped. "I know, baby, and I'm sorry. I did this. I should have had more restraint."

"Are you suggesting we shouldn't have hooked up?" she asked, her spine stiffening.

"Of course we shouldn't have hooked up. I knew that before we did it. That was never in question."

She blinked at him.

He continued, his shoulders relaxing a few inches. "However, I also know I couldn't have stopped myself. You cast a spell on me from the moment I saw you."

"So, it's my fault because I'm some sort of witch," she teased.

He shook his head. "No. It's my fault. I knew better. You offered me the apple. I took it. I could have said no."

She groaned. "Let's not compare this to original sin."

He chuckled. "Touché."

"And the blame game isn't doing any good either. We met. We had chemistry. We made memories."

"Are you sorry?" he asked.

She shook her head. "Not for a moment."

"Would you do it again?"

"In a heartbeat."

He swallowed, his expression serious. "Have you changed your mind about your willingness to date a SEAL?"

She wasn't sure if he was asking because he'd changed his or if he was taking her pulse to make sure they were still on the same page. "Have you changed your mind about dating at all?" It was a copout to answer his question with a question.

He glanced down at their hands again and squeezed hers as he spoke to the table. "I'm in the navy for life, Arianna. I would never ask someone to wait around for me, hoping I live and wondering when they might get two weeks of my time each year." He lifted his gaze. "Besides, it would be distracting to constantly be worrying about someone else's welfare. I made a commitment to myself never to get involved with a woman. I made a choice. I won't back down on that."

She nodded slowly again, a wave of emotions bombarding her. It was difficult to parse them out. He was right. She'd said all those same things to him on their first day together. Neither of them had gone into this thing blind. They had agreed they weren't interested in more than a fling, both of them citing the same exact reasons.

He was right, but what neither of them had factored into the equation was how hard they might fall for each other. This didn't feel like a fling. It felt like the real deal. When she closed her eyes during the quiet times in the middle of the night, she visualized the two of them together. In California, maybe. At her parents' for holidays, but living together. Maybe even raising a family together.

It was a pipe dream, but it had snuck into her psyche more than once in the past few days.

"Arianna?" he asked, one eyebrow raised. His grip had loosened, but he held her hand still.

She nodded. "You're right. Of course you're right. I haven't changed my mind. I don't want to be a woman left behind any more than you want to be the one leaving her. I made that deal with myself years before you made your own personal pact."

"But…"

"But, it's still complicated. I won't be able to lie about us. I'm not that good at deception. My mother, for one, will know with one glance at my face."

He chuckled. "Yeah. I believe that. So…we say we felt sparks, we spent some time together, and then decided in the end it didn't work out. Yeah?"

The lump that had grown larger in her throat for the past several days seemed too big to swallow past now. She didn't want to cry. There was no reason to. Why was she feeling so emotional? He had the perfect solution. The *only* solution. She nodded, pursing her lips.

With perfect timing, the waiter arrived with their wine.

# CHAPTER 17

The dinner was delicious. Every bite. They took their time, in no rush. Justus continued to seduce her throughout the meal, feeding her bites off his fork, stroking her skin at every opportunity, holding her gaze, kissing her fingers, rubbing his leg against hers.

It was perfect. Exactly how he'd planned it.

And yet, a cloud hung over him. A sharp pain pierced his heart. Their discussion had dampened the mood even though they didn't mention it again. In a few days he would leave her. They couldn't do this again. If they didn't sever ties and end things, they would ruin the entire definition of a fling.

He pondered the notion of planning to meet up with her at Christmas or on his next break, but that would only drag out the inevitable. By definition, any future plans would fall under the umbrella of a relationship. And they'd both agreed they didn't want to be in a relationship.

So, why did it hurt so bad?

When they got back to the hotel, they entered through

the front doors. Justus prayed their stalker wouldn't be lurking around, and he got lucky. He wasn't sure he could keep himself from punching the guy in the face if he stepped in their path that night.

By seemingly mutual agreement, they said nothing as the door to their room snicked shut behind them. Justus reverently cupped Arianna's face and kissed her. He let his hands slide down her body, taking in every curve. The feel of her breasts under the silky material made him moan into her mouth. He'd waited all night to cup them and stroke over the tight nipples that had taunted him all evening.

She shuddered at his touch, and he smoothed his hands down to her butt, molding his palms to her flesh beneath the dress before gathering the material with his fingers and easing it up. When his hands landed on her naked skin, she arched into him, driving him wild.

His cock had been stiff all day, but more so in the last few hours. He needed her. Slow and easy. Soft and gentle. But now.

Reaching between her legs, he drew a finger through her folds, finding her soaked. Had she spent the entire evening as aroused as he'd planned? He hoped so. He knew so.

She whimpered. "Justus," she murmured against his lips. "Don't make me wait any longer."

He would have loved to tease her for another hour, making her come over and over at his touch, but the truth was, he wasn't that strong. He needed to be inside her with a desperation that couldn't be explained in words. So, he whipped her dress over her head and draped it over the desk chair without looking.

She stood before him, gloriously naked except for her shoes and the strand of pearls at her throat.

"Lie on the bed. Legs wide. Keep the heels." She obeyed, taking her bottom lip between her teeth. A flush crawled up her chest and cheeks. So gorgeous. The color of her nipples deepened as they hardened. The short-cropped, dark curls at her sex glistened with arousal.

Slowly, Justus removed his tie and then unbuttoned his shirt. He never took his gaze off her delectable body. Under his scrutiny, she shuddered several times, but she kept her legs open, her heels planted against the mattress, the spikes digging into the sheet.

He shrugged out of his shirt, kicking off his shoes at the same time. His movements were more hurried as he divested himself of the rest of his clothes and then crawled up the bed to nestle himself between her legs. "Do you mind if I'm bare inside you again?" he asked as he met her gaze, stroking a lock of hair from her forehead.

"No." The word was breathy. She grabbed his biceps. "Please, Justus. I'm about to come without you touching me."

He smiled. "That was the plan."

"You succeeded. Don't make me wait any longer."

When she lifted her hips, he thrust into her, never losing her gaze.

She gasped, her mouth falling open as her eyes rolled back. "God, yes."

He visualized slowly making love to her, easing in and out until her nails dug into his arms. But she surprised him when she arched her head back and held her breath for less than a second before her orgasm washed through her.

*My God.* So beautiful. One thrust. Nothing but the contact of the base of his cock against her swollen clit.

Her body shook as the waves washed through her. His heart seized as he realized he'd fallen for her. Too deep. How the hell would he ever extricate himself from her?

The idea of walking away in a few days was impossible to grasp. And yet, he would have to find a way. She'd made it clear she didn't want to continue this relationship any more than he did.

When she resumed breathing, he pulled almost out and thrust back in. Her lips were still parted, her eyes glazed. And her nails indeed dug into his biceps. She was the entire package.

She was everything.

Justus awoke before Arianna again and spent several minutes staring at her profile as she lay on her belly, her head turned toward him. Her hair was smooth and thick, draped over one shoulder. He wanted to brush a lock from her cheek, but decided to watch her sleep instead, afraid he might wake her.

God, she was gorgeous. He'd gone to sleep knowing she was more than a fling, and now that he was awake, that realization burrowed itself deeper under his skin.

He had a serious problem on his hands and not a clue what to do about it. Leaving her didn't feel like an option. And yet it was the only option.

Suddenly, he felt restless. He needed to get out of this hotel room. Go for a run. Think. He needed oxygen to help clear his head.

He slid quietly from the bed without disturbing her and grabbed running shorts and a T-shirt from his suitcase. When he had his shoes on, he returned to her side, knowing he couldn't leave her without at least saying something.

His chest tightened as he stroked a finger down her

cheek and then leaned in to kiss her neck. She sighed as she rolled toward him, her small hand snaking out to settle on top of his. "Mmm. Why are you up?" she murmured, blinking her eyes open.

"Going for a run," he whispered. "You can go back to sleep." He kissed her cheek and then nuzzled her neck. She smelled so good. Like Arianna. Like his future. Like a future he'd sworn would never be his.

He needed to get out of this room before he ended up saying things he wasn't certain about.

She smiled as she snuggled back into the pillow. "'Kay."

He let his eyes close as he inhaled her scent one more time, and then he hurried from the room. He took the stairs to the ground floor, impatient to get on the street, too restless to wait for the elevator.

Finally, he was free of the building, jogging away, breathing deeply. He picked up his pace and forced himself to concentrate on putting one foot in front of the other. *Breathe*, he reminded himself over and over. Somehow there still wasn't enough oxygen outside either.

He was haunted by visuals of Arianna. Her smile. The tinkle of her laugh. The way her mouth fell open when she came. The soft moan she made. The way her eyes glazed over when he stroked her nipples.

*God.*

What the fuck was he going to do. How the hell was he going to leave her and return to life as if this vacation had never happened? It didn't seem possible.

Arianna couldn't fall back asleep after Justus left the room. Something about his departure felt off. He'd seemed different. Not his usual self. It shouldn't surprise her that he wanted to go for a run. After all, in his normal life he worked out nearly every day, and so far he hadn't left her side for a week to do anything physical.

Not that they didn't work out hard between the sheets every day more than once. She smiled and stared at the ceiling. No way could she go back to sleep now, so she slid from the bed and padded to the bathroom.

A half hour later she was dressed and ready to start the day. She assumed Justus would return soon. How far did the man intend to run? She sat in the chair next to the desk and picked up her phone. Almost immediately, it rang in her hand. The call was unknown, but she answered it anyway. "Hello?"

"Hey. It's me." He sounded out of breath.

"Did you get lost?" she teased.

"Nope. But I went farther than I intended. I'm heading back now, but it will take me a while. Or I could grab a cab."

A knock sounded at the door, making Arianna jump. "Hang on a second. Someone's at the door." She set the phone on the desk next to her purse and crossed to the door. Without thought, she opened it, expecting to see housekeeping.

The man standing in the hallway was not there to clean the room. "Chris?" She smiled at him. "What are you doing here?"

He rocked back and forth on his feet, his fingers tucked into his pockets. "I'm heading to Sydney today. Thought I'd see if you guys wanted to grab breakfast or coffee before I leave." He leaned on the doorjamb.

Arianna nearly laughed out loud. Justus had probably been right. If Chris somehow managed to get them to pay for breakfast, the bet, such as it was, was over. But they had the money, so who cared if she bought this guy breakfast. "Come on in. I was just about to go downstairs and grab breakfast in the hotel. Let me get my purse."

Chris stepped inside and glanced around. "Where's Justus?"

"He went for a run. He can meet us in the restaurant when he gets back." As she spun around to grab her purse from the desk, her mind was on the bet she had with Justus. Her brain was going through different scenarios, wondering what would happen when the bill came if she didn't readily offer to pay.

She reached for her purse, suddenly remembering she'd left Justus on the phone. As she reached for it, intending to apologize to him and fill him in on the breakfast plan, she came up short.

Chris wrapped his fingers around her forearm, too tightly. He also stepped closer to her than necessary. His voice was low and filled with menace when he spoke, his tone totally wrong, not resembling anything she'd ever heard from him before. "Do you have any idea how frustrating it's been waiting for you to be alone without that giant Neanderthal attached to your hip?" He pressed his chest into her back.

She gasped. "What are you talking about?" she asked, her hands shaking as she stared at the desk where her phone rested, praying the line remained open, grateful she'd left it face down. Something was very, very wrong.

He released her to step to her side, his hands on his hips, and rolled his eyes. "Don't play coy with me. Let's go."

"Go?" *What the hell?* "Go where?"

"To the bank, you stupid bitch. You got yourself a windfall, and I need that money."

147

Her eyes bugged out. How could he know about the reward money? "What money?"

Chris, or whoever he was, narrowed his gaze and gritted his teeth. "Grab your purse. We're going to take a nice little trip to the bank. If you withdraw the money like a good girl, I'll let you live. If you give me any trouble, your fuckbuddy will never find your body." He turned toward the door. "Let's go."

Chris pulled a long knife out of a sheath beneath his shirt and held it up for her to see. "It's sharp. If you want me to, I can kill you now, take your bank information myself, and withdraw the money without you. It won't be as tidy, but I'll do it. You won't be the first stupid, gullible bitch I've killed."

She swallowed, shaking her head. "Put the knife away. I'll go with you. I don't care about the money. If you need it so badly, it's yours."

He chuckled. Sardonically. His voice was all wrong. He was a good actor.

Justus had been right. All along.

While he resheathed the knife, she swept her phone into her purse and then picked up the strap and settled it over her shoulder. *God, please tell me Justus is still on the line and can hear everything.*

It was her only hope. She truly didn't care about the damn money, but would Chris leave her alive after he had his hands on it, or would he kill her anyway?

She was shaking as she stepped into the hallway with him, and she gasped when he grabbed her arm roughly and yanked her toward the exit sign where the stairs were located. Of course he wouldn't risk the elevator.

He kept her close to his side, hissing words into her ear through gritted teeth. "You would be wise to pretend we're a couple and do as I say. Got it?"

"Yes," she muttered. *Justus, are you listening?* Their conversation would be muffled in her purse. She crossed her arms under her chest and tried to hold her purse open slightly with her fingers. "Where are we going?"

"There's a branch of your bank nearby."

"How did you know about the money?" she asked as they took the stairs at a rapid pace. "I never mentioned it."

He chuckled again, that deep, grating sound that would haunt her for the rest of her life, if she lived. "I was in the station in Sydney when you came to collect."

She jerked her gaze to his, her eyes wide. "What? How?"

He shrugged, his fingers digging into her arm as he continued to manhandle her down the next flight of stairs. "Got picked up for drugs that night. Watched the entire play-by-play between you and that old lady with the diamond. It was kind of you to leave an itinerary on the officer's desk."

Arianna realized Chris's accent had changed. It no longer had the same distinctive lilt. He wasn't from New Zealand at all. He was Australian. Obviously, he also didn't have a fiancée who left him at the altar, nor was he on his honeymoon. God, she was dense. If she somehow got out of this mess, she would never doubt Justus's instincts again.

She nearly sobbed.

"I'd give almost anything to see the look on that asshole's face when he finds you missing from the room. Your boyfriend never leaves you alone for a second." He glanced up and down her body as he shoved the door open to the outside, smirking. "Though I can't say as I blame him. You are one hot chick. No wonder he keeps a close eye on you."

She suddenly had an idea that might come in handy. "He's not my boyfriend."

149

Chris furrowed his brow, his grip on her arm having eased as they stepped outside and headed down the sidewalk. "What the fuck are you talking about?"

"You weren't the only one who lied." She leaned closer to him. "I don't even know for sure if Justus is his real name. I just met him the day you saw us."

Chris stopped walking and turned to face her. "What the fuck?" he repeated.

She shrugged, trying to remain calm. "It's true. Do I look like I would have any more money than you do? I saw him at a bar the day before you saw us and laid on the flirting until he picked me up. It was too easy to take advantage of him." She tried to sound casual. "Hot, sexy man traveling alone from the States. I didn't figure I would get more out of it than amazing sex and a nice vacation, but then we got that money. Win-win. I pretended I was Julia Roberts in *Pretty Woman*." She forced herself to giggle, but God, it was hard.

Chris slowly smirked. "Fuck me."

"You might have noticed I wasn't the one who actually found the ring or deserved the reward, but I was the only one who had a bank account. That sucker didn't even mind if I deposited it. I guess he's rich or something." She stared directly into Chris's eyes, hoping she was convincing. Making up a giant lie was not her thing, but her life depended on it.

He chuckled. "I'm losing my touch."

*You're losing way more than your touch, buddy.* "That money wasn't even mine to begin with. How about if we withdraw it and you take me with you? I'm kind of tired of the brooding Justus anyway."

Chris sobered and narrowed his gaze. "I don't need a woman with me."

"Whatever. Doesn't matter to me. If you'll give me half, I'll get lost."

He stared at her a moment and then turned to drag her down the sidewalk again. "We'll see."

# CHAPTER 18

Justus was out of his mind. He was also kicking himself in the ass as he ran down the beach as fast as he could until he reached a spot where he could jump onto the sidewalk. He should have linked their phones on the first day so he could track her now. He was a fucking Navy SEAL for God's sake. Why the hell had he taken this kind of risk? This was Arianna Gallo. Tony's sister.

Contrary to the crazy tale she was feeding Chris, she was the most important person in Justus's life. He would never be able to forgive himself if anything happened to her. Not on his watch. Not on anyone's watch. Not ever.

His chest pounded as he ran as hard as he could, paying no attention to anyone in the vicinity. He somehow managed to hold the phone close to his ear to catch her conversation all the while. However, he needed to lower it a few inches and switch screens so he could find every branch of her bank in the area. If he chose wrong, she might pay with her life.

He typed in her bank and then watched as pins fell all over the screen. "Fuck," he muttered, nearly knocking into a woman with a stroller. He ignored her glare and kept jogging. There were several branches of that bank. He zoomed in to figure out which one was closest to the hotel.

Luckily, that paid off. "Bingo." He dashed catty-corner to jaywalk across the street, aiming for the branch he hoped Chris was taking Arianna to.

Holding the phone to his ear again, he tried to grasp anything Arianna might say. She obviously knew the phone line was open, and she was trying to slow things down.

And then his woman got even smarter. "Mulgrave Road? My bank isn't on Mulgrave Road. We're going the wrong way."

Chris laughed. "There are a several branches. The Lake Street branch is too small."

"Good job, baby," he whispered to himself, picking up the pace. Shit. He was ten minutes away if he ran hard. Thank God he was wearing tennis shoes and track shorts.

This was the first time he'd left Arianna during the entire trip. Now, he could kick himself for leaving her for even an hour. He'd known Chris Metz was bad news. He'd known it from the moment the man approached them. He'd also had the suspicion that he'd seen him somewhere before. And apparently he was right. The fucking police station in Sydney. This asshole had been following them from that moment forward.

Hell, he hadn't needed to follow them. The fucker had picked up their itinerary and tracked them from place to place. It had been too easy.

Meanwhile, Justus had been so consumed with Arianna that he hadn't paid close enough attention to his surroundings. He was a fucking SEAL. People didn't usually get the jump on him.

Of course he'd also never been in a situation like this

where he was so consumed with another human being that he let his guard down. *Run faster.*

Voices filled the open line, indicating to Justus they'd probably entered the bank. He glanced at the GPS. It said he was still seven minutes away on foot. Except Justus wasn't walking, nor was he following straight lines. He could do it in three minutes. No way could anything happen to Arianna in three minutes inside a bank, right?

"Yes. Hi. I'd like to make a withdraw from my account."

Silence. Justus wondered how much money she'd put down and how shocked the teller might be.

"A withdraw you say, ma'am?"

"Yes. Please."

*Please, baby. Please tell me your winking at that woman or giving her a sign of some sort. Please.*

"No problem. I'll just need to grab some paperwork for you to fill out for a sum that large. I'll be right back."

"Thank you."

*Blessed angels. Paperwork, my ass.* The woman knew.

Justus rounded the last corner. He could see the bank a few blocks in front of him. He picked up the pace. If he was lucky, a police car would arrive soon too. If not, he prayed this fucker didn't have a gun. In either case, Justus was about to fuck up his day.

"If you'll just come with me, ma'am," the teller stated. "You can have a seat in the first office on the right while someone handles the transaction for you."

"Thank you so much," Arianna said.

*First office on the right…* Justus jumped over the last curb and took the stairs leading to the front door of the bank three at a time. He flew through the door just as he noticed flashing lights in his peripheral vision. Good.

The moment he stepped inside the open lobby area, he scanned the offices on both sides. He spotted Arianna immediately. But Chris also lifted his gaze at that moment. The man jumped to his feet, grabbed Arianna by the arm, and hauled her to standing.

Arianna screamed as Justus closed the distance.

Chris put her in front of him, pulled a knife out of his waistband, and pressed it against her neck.

Justus slammed into the room through the glass door, letting it hit the far wall, a loud clanging of the metal frame surely drawing the attention of everyone in the bank. Justus made eye contact with Arianna long enough to reassure himself she wasn't injured. He jerked his gaze upward. "Put the knife down, asshole. You're in a fucking bank. There is no way to escape. The cops are right on my tail."

"Drop your weapon," someone shouted authoritatively from behind Justus. "Now."

Justus crept closer, hands open in front of him. "Let her go, man. You don't want to do this. If you hurt her, you'll be in way more trouble than you are now." Justus stopped walking, hoping he was convincing Chris to do the right thing. He was only three feet away. He could take Chris down in an instant. The only reason he hadn't made his move was because he was hoping to avoid the possibility of Arianna getting injured in the process.

All his training kicked in. This was a hostage situation. The only difference was this hostage was his own woman, not a stranger. Nevertheless, he was trained to take down an assailant in this kind of situation. He'd done so, many times. He needed to keep his head on straight and focus.

*Follow protocol.*

"Fuck you. Back off," Chris shouted, spittle hitting Arianna in the face. He backed into the wall, dragging Arianna with him.

She whimpered, her hands going to his forearm. Her eyes were wide and wild.

"Let her go," Justus repeated.

"Drop the knife," the officer at his back shouted again.

The second Chris shifted his gaze from Justus to the officer, Justus made his move. Lunging forward, he lifted one hand and slammed his palm into the man's forehead. At the same time, he wrapped his palm around the man's fist on the knife and jerked it away from Arianna's neck.

Chris went down hard, dazed. He stumbled to the left and slumped to the floor.

Arianna screamed, backing away from Chris into the corner of the room. Her hands were at her throat.

Justus, assured Chris was out cold and confident the officer rushing past him had things under control, turned toward Arianna.

She still held her neck, but there was no blood oozing around her fingers.

Justus closed the distance in less than a second, hauling her against his chest. He threaded his hand in her hair and held her tight. "You're okay." He turned her away from Chris and cupped her face, tilting her head back so he could look into her eyes. "You're okay," he repeated.

Tears ran down her face, and she sucked in a breath and sobbed. Her hands went to his forearms. "He threatened to kill me."

"I know, baby. But I'm here. I've got you."

She cried harder. "Why didn't I listen to you?"

The room was filling with people. Justus ignored them. "Because you're kind and trusting."

She swallowed. "I'm stupid."

He shook his head. "You're not. You're human."

"You told me over and over again. I ignored you."

"Arianna, this is far more my fault than yours. I should

have done something. I shouldn't have left you alone. I suspected and yet I let it go on and on. I've never ignored my instincts like that."

Another sob. Tears were streaming down her cheeks.

Justus rubbed them with his thumbs. "You're safe now," he repeated.

"Sir? I'm going to need to ask you two a few questions." The voice came from Justus's right.

"Of course. Can we get my girlfriend out of this room, please?" He didn't want her to have to look at the man on the ground who was now coming to and groaning.

"Yes. Follow me."

Justus followed the officer. He was about an inch shorter than Justus with dark skin and hair. He wasted no time leading the two of them around the corner where Arianna wouldn't be able to easily see Chris.

Justus could still hear the man, but he stood between Arianna and the bank office. It was comprised of a wall of glass, so it would be nearly impossible to prevent a glimpse.

"Can you tell me what happened?" the officer asked, his gaze on Arianna's.

Arianna nodded and took a deep breath. She retold every step of the event from the moment she'd set the phone down in the hotel room until Justus arrived at the bank. She left out no details. Justus would never forget the entire trauma, considering he'd been forced to listen to the woman who owned his heart living it through the open phone line.

When she was finished, Justus explained where he'd come from and how he'd found her. He wrote down all their information and took a card from the officer. "You're a lucky woman today," he told Arianna with a smile. "I'd hang on to this one. **Never** hurts to have a SEAL on your side when you get in a bind."

Arianna wiped away more tears with the backs of her hands. "Thank you."

"Don't thank me. Thank the teller who was sharp enough to realize you were here under duress." The officer stepped away.

Justus wrapped an arm around Arianna's shoulders and led her away from the room where several officers still stood over Chris's body, though Justus was certain the man's name wasn't Chris. "How did you warn the teller?" Justus asked.

She smiled up at him. "I spelled my name wrong on the form. Two r's and one n. Apparently it worked. I didn't care if she thought I had stolen my own identity as long as she called the police."

Justus pulled her closer to his chest and kissed the top of her head. "Smart move, baby." He had a lot of things to say to her. Thousands. But not here. Not in this bank. Not while people were listening. Not while she was shaking so badly she couldn't focus.

# CHAPTER 19

When Arianna stepped into the shower two hours later, she was still shaking. Even standing under the hot water didn't calm her nerves enough to keep her from shivering.

Luckily, Justus followed her into the enclosure and wrapped his arms around her middle, keeping her upright, her back against his front. He smoothed her wet hair away from her face and held on tight, his lips on her ear. "I changed our flight to tomorrow."

She sobbed, unable to keep the sound from escaping.

"I've got you, baby. Deep breaths." He rocked her back and forth, somehow sharing his strength while she cried. When she was finally drained of tears, he reached for the soap and washed her, never letting go, never putting space between them, never ceasing his constant reassurances that she was okay.

Justus helped her from the shower and grabbed a towel, wrapping it around her body as he pulled her into his embrace for the millionth time.

Her hair was dripping, but somehow he managed to pat her curls with a second towel, leaving them damp. "I still don't know how you get this hair straight every day," he said as he fingered through the locks.

"Magic," she said, tipping her head back to meet his gaze. "Hairdryer, really. And a lot of product." She knew he was trying to distract her by changing the subject. It was working. She was drained. Her fear had ebbed. She was breathing far more normally, finally.

"I bet it looks nice if you just leave it natural."

She smiled. "Well, it's not nearly as out of control as it was when I was fourteen. Much less frizzy. But I've gotten in the habit of wearing it straight. No one has seen it curly in years, except when I swim."

"*I* have." He stroked her face. "In the ocean and the shower and in bed." He kissed her nose. "Leave it. Let me see what it looks like when it dries."

She shrugged. "If you want."

He bent down and lifted her off the ground.

She squealed as he carried her from the room. "What are you doing?"

"Didn't want to stand in the bathroom all day." He sat on the edge of the bed and swung them around until his back was to the headboard and she sat on his lap.

For a long time she curled into him, snuggling close, trying to keep from shaking. "I have to call my parents," she finally stated.

"I know."

"They'll freak out if they find out I was abducted by knife and didn't tell them."

"I know," he repeated, kissing the top of her head again. "You want me to call them?"

She sat up straighter, meeting his gaze. "You?"

"Yes."

"And say what? Aren't you worried they're already going to be furious with you?"

Justus licked his lips, holding her gaze. His expression was serious.

Her heart skipped a beat. What the hell was he about to say? She was confident he was about to break her heart. A heart that never should have been available for breaking in the first place.

Not only had she been responsible for her own abduction today because she wouldn't listen to his reasoning when all kinds of alarms went off in his head, but she'd also managed to fall in love with him. She was a fool. And he knew it.

Justus suddenly turned to one side and set her next to him. He gave her body a tug so that she ended up flat on her back, the towel still tucked around her. He hovered over her, his gaze so damn serious, she couldn't breathe. She was about to get a lecture she didn't want to hear.

"I fucked up," he began.

"No, you didn't—"

He set two fingers over her lips. "Please. Hear me out."

She nodded, her eyes wide with concern.

He stroked her lips and then released them. "I told you I didn't want a girlfriend. I told you we could only have these ten days. I agreed with you when you said you didn't want to date anyone in the military anyway."

She swallowed. Where was he going with this? A fresh tear escaped. She was so damn emotional today.

"I promised myself I would not let this thing between us become more than a fling. Ten days. Nothing more."

She still didn't move. Now, she didn't breathe either. Another tear slid down her cheek.

His voice dipped lower, his gaze holding hers. "I promised myself I would not fall in love with you."

She sucked in a sharp breath.

"I fucked up the plan, and I'm sorry. When that asshole

took you…" He inhaled slowly, seemingly trying to control his emotions. His eyes slid shut for a moment. His voice came out softer and slower. "When he took you, my world came to a halt. My heart stopped beating. I've never been so scared in my life. Not even on the front lines. Not even when hunting down an enemy in the dark in a foreign country."

She opened her mouth, but she still didn't know how to respond. She wasn't even sure what he was trying to say.

He continued. "I'm in love with you, Arianna. Head over heels. I didn't mean for it to happen. It just did. And there's no way to make it stop. I knew it before I called you. I planned to come back to the hotel and beg you to give us a chance. And then…" He paused, taking a deep breath. "I know I said I never wanted a girlfriend because I didn't want to spend my days worrying about someone else when I need my head in the game, but the truth is, it's too late now. It wouldn't matter if I did walk away and leave you. You're under my skin anyway."

More tears slid down. A stream of them. *He's in love with me?*

"You're in my heart. I know you've spent your life adamant about not dating military personnel, and I'll respect your wishes if you ask me to walk away." He lifted her hand and rubbed her knuckles against his cheek.

"Justus…" she finally managed.

But he shook his head and kept talking. "The thing is, it won't change anything. It's done. You're in my soul. Whether or not you accept me in your life, you'll still be in mine. You'll forever be in my thoughts. You'll be the first thing I think about in the morning and the last thing I think about at night." He closed his eyes tight for a moment and then reopened them. "I don't even have a single picture of you on my phone because I was too stubborn to take one."

That made her smile through the falling tears. "I could send you some from my phone."

He returned the smile. "I'm hoping you've fallen just as hard for me too. I think you have. Have you?"

*Holy shit.* This was happening. She was totally in love with this amazing man, and he was in love with her.

He pursed his lips and set his forehead against hers. "Say something." His grip was tight on her fingers, still pressed against his cheek.

"You navy boys make life so freaking complicated."

He didn't move, not even to take his gaze away from hers.

She smiled at him. "You're going to leave me for months at a time and scare the hell out of me daily and I'll be worrying if you're alive or dead."

"Yeah. I will."

"I'm going to become one of those damn military girlfriends who cries over tea and drinks with the other women at night to chase away the loneliness."

"I know. I'm sorry."

More tears fell. They were happy tears now, but he couldn't know that. "I miss you already," she whispered.

"Say it."

She glanced at his lips.

He squeezed her hand. "Say it, baby. I need to hear you say it."

"I love you."

His lips were on hers in an instant, her head angling to the side to totally consume her. He moaned into her mouth, his tongue tangling with hers, urgent, demanding. He kissed her forever.

When he finally broke free, he was gasping for breath. "My God. I'm so in love with you I can't see straight."

She met his gaze. His eyes were dancing with happiness. A happiness she mirrored. "It's a blurry experience. You're right."

"Tell me you feel the same way." He seemed to need reassurance. In fact, he rose to straddle her, coming down on his hands and knees above her. His towel gaping open.

She lifted her hands to his face. "Justus, I've been in love with you for a decade. This week just solidified the fact. I've been lying to myself for days."

"You're mine?"

She chuckled. "I'm totally yours. I've always been yours."

"I swear I'll do the best I can by you. I know it won't be easy, but I'll work harder than anyone you've ever known." He cupped her face with one hand.

She set her fingers over the back of his hand and drew it to her lips to kiss his palm. "You don't have to do anything except look at me the way you're looking at me now every time I see you."

He smiled wider. "That won't be difficult. You take my breath away." He reached for the front of her towel. "Before we call your parents, can I please make love to you?"

She grabbed the spot where the towel came together. "Not a chance. Don't forget you won a bet. You'll be enjoying a nice lap dance from a woman in sexy lingerie before you get to have sex tonight."

His brows rose along with one side of his mouth. "Where you gonna get the lingerie? Because I'm not leaving this room again today. I already changed our flight. If we get hungry, there's always room service. So, I guess I'll have to take a rain check on that sexy dance."

She smiled broader. "I bought the teddy you requested while I was buying the dress. Sorry. You didn't get to choose the color."

He rose up above her on his knees, his eyes dancing with excitement. "Tell me you're not kidding."

"I'm not kidding. It's in my suitcase. If you let me up, I'll put it on."

He stared down at her for a long time, searching her face. "Damn, you're amazing. Why did you think you would lose the bet? You couldn't have known."

She smoothed her hands up his abs. "Justus, I never cared about the stupid bet. I just wanted to make memories with you. This one is going to be the best one yet."

"There is no doubt about that, but I want to fully enjoy every second, so we should call your parents first."

She winced. "Must we?" How had the tables turned? "What time is it in Rome right now?"

He shrugged. "I don't know, but we have to call them anyway. They'll kill both of us if we don't let them know what happened today and that you're okay." He scrambled off the bed. "I'll do it. Where is your phone?"

Arianna pushed to sitting while she let Justus place the call. She chewed on her lower lip, knees pulled up to her chest. He put the phone on speaker and set it on the bed between them while it was still ringing.

Her mother answered on the third ring. "Arianna?"

"Hey, Mom."

"You've got me on the line too, Mrs. Gallo. Justus."

"Justus." Her voice perked up. "You know better than to call me Mrs. Gallo. Please. Call me Maryanne."

Justus sat on the edge of the bed, grinning. "Of course, Mrs. Gallo."

Her mother laughed. "How is your vacation going? Tony told me you two had a packed itinerary."

Justus smirked.

Arianna rolled her eyes. Of course Tony told her.

"We're having a marvelous time, actually," Justus began, "however, we did run into a bit of trouble this morning. That's why we're calling."

"What happened?" Her voice rose. There was a rustling noise, and then Arianna heard her father's voice on the phone. Her mother had put them on speaker.

"Arianna? Honey? What's going on?" he boomed.

"Sir, this is Justus. We were just about to explain. A man has been following us for several days. He had the intention of robbing Arianna. So, he was watching as I left the room this morning to go for a run. He took advantage of my absence and forced Arianna to go to the bank with him."

Arianna's father, Enzo, sucked in a sharp breath.

Maryanne gasped. "My God. He kidnapped her?"

Arianna cringed, knowing Justus had specifically avoided that word. "I'm fine, Mom. He tried. He was unsuccessful."

Justus cleared his throat. "Your daughter is very resourceful, Mrs. Gallo. She did everything right, including keeping me on the phone the entire time and alerting the bank teller. I beat the police to the bank, in fact."

"Arianna?" her mother cried out. "That's so scary. Are you sure you're okay?"

"Honey, I'm worried about you," her father added.

"I'm fine. Justus is with me. I was freaked out. He calmed me down. It's over now. The perpetrator is in custody." She reached for Justus's hand and squeezed it.

Her mother breathed heavily for several seconds. "Why don't you come to Rome, sweetie, or at least meet us back in New York next week?"

"Because I have two more months here. I'll be fine. I promise."

"But isn't Justus leaving in a few days?"

Justus grinned. "I am, ma'am, but I'll make sure Arianna is safe before I leave. It was a fluke. She'll be safely back at work in Sydney before I get on a plane."

"Okay…" Her mother didn't sound convinced. "When are *you* coming back to New York?" she asked.

Arianna winced, knowing she was talking to Justus.

"I don't know yet, Mrs. Gallo. As soon as I can." He met Arianna's gaze and held it. Seconds passed while they stared at each other, both knowing the next few months and possibly years were going to be difficult. Also knowing they had no choice. They would make it work. They would find a way.

"Arianna? Are you still there?"

Arianna jerked her gaze back to the phone. "Yes. Sorry, Mom. I'm here. Please don't let anyone worry. I'll be in touch in a few days."

"Okay, honey, but be careful. Justus?"

"Ma'am?"

"Make sure my daughter is safe."

"I will do my best. She's important to me."

Arianna's heart swelled as he made that announcement. She knew it would be huge for her mother. Just a few little words that would change everything.

She heard her mother's sharp intake of breath. "I assumed as much." Arianna could hear a sob in her mother's voice. "When Tony told us you were going to Australia during your leave…" Her voice trailed off.

Arianna closed her eyes and leaned into Justus. Tony might not have realized he'd inadvertently set the two of them up, but her mother wasn't stupid.

Her father cleared his throat. "Be safe. Love you both."

"Thanks, Pop. Bye, Mom."

"Bye, Mr. and Mrs. Gallo." Justus reached over to tap the phone and end the call. He tossed the phone on the nightstand and crawled toward Arianna, stalking her. "How many minutes before Tony calls, do you think?"

"We placing a bet on this too?"

Justus laughed. "Depends. What are we wagering this time? I haven't even collected my last debt."

"Do you think he'll be surprised when he finds out we're together?" She was grinning.

Justus winced. "I still think he'll kick my ass, but eventually he'll have to get over it."

"He might have been oblivious, but my mother knew I had a crush on you," she pointed out. "When he told her you were coming here for your leave, I'm sure she suspected I would work my ass off to get you to see me. Doesn't mean she'll tell Tony. You might be forced to handle that on your own."

Justus reached out and grabbed her, hauling her against his body. "I'll handle Tony. And, by the way, you didn't have to do anything to get me to see you. My eyes were wide open the second I walked up to you." He kissed her gently.

"I feel like I hit the lottery."

"Hmmm. Baby, the lottery winner is me."

# CHAPTER 20

Justus was still sitting on the bed, leaning against the headboard, while he waited for Arianna to emerge from the bathroom. He'd seen her naked body enough times that he thought it was a little silly for her to change from her naked self in a towel to whatever lingerie she'd purchased behind a closed door, but perhaps she was right. The suspense was making his dick hard while he wondered if she would have gone with white or black.

His cock went from hard to painfully stiff the second she emerged. His breath also left his lungs. She hadn't gone with white or black. She'd gone with red. A deep blood red that made his mouth water the moment she stepped into view. She also had on strappy red heels. "Jesus," he murmured. "You sure know how to kill a man."

She giggled. "I hope you don't die just because I'm wearing something sexy. That would spoil years of fun."

He licked his lips. "Baby, that is way beyond sexy, and I like the way you're thinking. Years and years of fun."

She stalked around the room seductively. "Especially if

all we get is two-week increments like this. We'll have to plan well and take advantage of every moment."

The thought of only seeing her a few weeks at a time for years did not sit well. He had no idea how to process that, but right now wasn't the time. Right now he was trying to get his eyes to blink even though he would miss those precious moments of vision.

He leaned forward with the intention of snagging her by the hand and hauling her closer.

She jumped back. "Uh-uh. Sit back. Let me tease."

"Tease happened in the first few seconds. I'm so hard I'm going to come while you're strutting around the room." He opened the towel and took his dick in his hand, hoping the sight would entice her to approach, maybe straddle him.

"Hands off your cock, big guy. Put them next to your hips."

He totally stopped breathing. Did she just give an order?

He stared at her, his hand stilling.

She lifted a brow. "Let it go, Justus. Hands to your sides. I want to watch your cock react to me on its own."

For a heartbeat, he hesitated, and then he decided this game was beyond fun. It was a dream come true. Granted, two could play. So if she thought it was a good idea to boss him around while she teased him to death, she would find herself in quite a dire situation next time he was in control.

Sure, he'd made her sweat it out the day before, denying her orgasms while the desire built all day, but there was so much more he could do to drive her crazy with need if she didn't mind a little bondage play or perhaps even some toys.

Never in his wildest imagination would he have

expected to be turned on by having a woman order him around, but this was Arianna. She could do anything she wanted. She owned his heart.

And she was hotter than hell in that red teddy. It was little more than strips of lace and a bit of silk in between. Her dark skin teased him between the fabric. And her nipples were equally visible between the dainty lace at her breasts.

He licked his lips again.

She picked up her phone and tapped the screen a few times. He certainly hoped she was turning it off. Tony hadn't called yet. It was too late now. No way was Justus taking a call from his best friend for at least another hour.

When soft music filled the room, Justus realized what she'd been doing. His cock jumped against his belly as she moved to the music. So sensual. He'd had no idea she could dance. Then again, maybe dance wasn't the right word for the seductive way she was slinking around, using every piece of furniture to tease him with a variety of positions.

Every time she bent over or lifted her leg behind her, he gulped. She gave him a show he would never forget.

By the time she finally climbed onto the mattress and crawled toward him on her hands and knees, he was speechless. Her breasts hung swollen, her nipples tight buds. The only part of her he hadn't gotten a good look at yet was the exact spot he most adored between her legs.

She didn't seem in a mood to give him that just yet either. No. Her gaze was on his cock. And her crawl was aimed toward the bobbing appendage.

He fisted his hands at his sides next to his hips.

She straddled his legs, making him groan, but instead of climbing the rest of the way up his body, she lowered her face to his dick and licked a line from the base to the tip.

He groaned. "Baby..."

"Mmm."

*Jesus.*

Two seconds later, her lips were wrapped around his length, and she sucked him deep and hard without pausing. No hands. Just her mouth. Her fucking sexy curls fell all around her face, curtaining her and adding to the allure. If she never straightened her hair again, he would be fine. It was hot straight, but in his opinion, it was even sexier natural, curls everywhere.

She set her hands on his thighs while she tortured him with her mouth.

He gritted his teeth, willing to let her play for about ten more seconds before he turned the tables.

In painstakingly slow motion, she lifted off his cock and sucked him back down. Deeper this time.

That was it. He didn't want to come in her mouth. Not this time.

He lunged forward, grabbed her by the waist, and flipped her onto her back.

She gasped, a giggle escaping her mouth. "Hey, I wasn't done."

"Yes, you were." He claimed her mouth in a hard, demanding kiss until she moaned. God, he loved that sound. With her hands on his back, her nails digging into his skin, he lowered one hand to her core and explored.

He froze when he reached between her legs, lifting his gaze to stare down at her. "Imp." He crawled down her body, spreading her legs, and settling between them. Two surprises had caught his attention. One, she'd shaved. Bare.

*Fuck me.*

And two, the teddy was split right up the center. Crotchless, in a sense. Her glistening folds were wide open to him. He stroked a finger through her moisture, eliciting a gasp as her eyes rolled back. She was so ready for him, and he needed his mouth on her urgently, more than he needed his cock inside her.

She whimpered as he withdrew his fingers and then slid down her body. Before she could react, his hands were on her thighs, pressing them wide, his lips on her sweet center. He didn't have the patience to ease into his assault. Desperation controlled his movements. He sucked her pussy into his mouth and thrust his tongue into her channel.

She cried out, her hips stiffening as they lifted toward him. Her hands landed on his head. "Justus," she breathed.

He withdrew his tongue from her tightness to flick it rapidly over her clit.

"Oh God." Her voice was shrill.

He wanted her to come against his mouth. He wanted to swallow her orgasm while he continued to torment her toward a second one, but his cock was too hard, too insistent. He released her abruptly, scrambled up her body, lined his cock up with her entrance, and thrust home.

She screamed. Loudly. "Oh, God. Justus. Oh, God."

He loved that sound. And he made her do it again two seconds later on his next thrust. And again. And again. In a few moments her throat elongated, her lips slackened, and then she came. So beautiful. Her hair spread out against the pillow. Her hands gripping his back. Her hips lifted off the bed.

Perfection.

*Mine.*

Forever.

Without moving a muscle, he too came, deep and hard, so hot for her that he knew this lust between them would never fade. Not in a million years.

He had no idea how he was going to fix things so that

her future didn't match the sorrowful picture she had in her mind, but he would find a way. And he would make it happen.

## CHAPTER 21

*Three months later...*

Arianna rushed into the living room of her brother Tony's San Diego apartment, carrying her sandals. Tony's fiancée, Darcy, was sitting on the couch staring at her phone. "Sorry I'm running late." The two of them had lunch plans, and then they were going to see an early movie.

Arianna had been back in the States a month. She'd spent the first two weeks with her parents in New York, but she'd come to San Diego two weeks ago, and she was staying at Tony's place with Darcy while she looked for a job.

Darcy had only recently moved to San Diego herself to be with Tony. She'd insisted she would love to have Arianna stay with her. The two of them could commiserate together. Keep each other company while Tony and Justus were deployed.

Justus had told Arianna she was welcome to stay at *his* apartment, even insisting at times, but Arianna hadn't been comfortable moving into his place when he wasn't home himself. Besides, she knew she would be lonely, and wandering around in his space would make things worse. She would wait for him to get home, and then they could discuss her living arrangements. For now, she was content to stay with Darcy. They both were.

Arianna's life was upside down, but she'd known from the moment Justus had left Australia that she needed to relocate to San Diego where he would be stationed when he wasn't deployed.

"No worries. I'm not in a hurry," Darcy assured her. "The movie doesn't start for two hours. We've got plenty of time."

Arianna sighed, trying to slow her racing heart. She was exhausted lately. And truthfully, a little frustrated.

She took a deep breath and plopped down on the couch to put her sandals on. Her skirt spread out around her.

Darcy met her gaze when she was finished. "You okay?"

Arianna leaned back on the sofa. "I think so." She tucked a curly lock of hair behind her ear, wondering for the millionth time why the hell she'd stopped straightening her hair to appease a man she hadn't seen in three months.

"I know it's stressful. This isn't a life we would choose."

"Yeah." She sighed. Most of the time the two of them tried to pretend everything was normal. Sometimes, they paused for a serious moment.

"You can do this. It's in your blood. Half your cousins are married to the military."

Adrianna groaned. "God, don't remind me, and please don't use the M-word. I'm barely existing as a peripheral girlfriend right now. Let's not talk marriage. He's starting to seem like an apparition, like I dreamed him up, and those ten days never happened."

Darcy smiled warmly. "I'm pretty sure they happened.

And I'm pretty sure you know this is it for you, or you wouldn't have relocated to San Diego."

Darcy was right about that. There was no way to ignore her feelings for Justus, which was why she'd agreed to this arrangement in the first place. It wouldn't even do any good to break up with him because it wouldn't change her heart.

She'd done okay while she was finishing her last two months in Australia. She spoke to him through FaceTime every few days, and he was fantastic with email, often sending her more than one to look forward to while she slept.

Since returning to the States and moving in with Tony's fiancée, she'd been antsy. She'd meant to get a job at one of the major hotels as soon as possible. She'd even had an interview. But her life felt like it was on hold. And that was frustrating.

Being committed to a SEAL was demanding. It required flexibility. It wasn't conducive to her getting a sixty-hour-a-week job because the reality was that when Justus did surface, she wanted to be with him every moment.

Was she crazy? Her life was in limbo. She was living in her brother's apartment. And her "boyfriend" was a man she hardly knew whom she'd spent ten magical days with three months ago.

Okay. That wasn't exactly fair. She knew him better than she admitted to herself. She'd known him for years. They'd spent countless hours talking on the phone in the last three months. She knew what kind of man he was. And any questions she had about him could easily be answered by Tony.

Of course, Tony hadn't been home more than a few days in three months either.

Arianna forced herself to respond to Darcy's comment. "I'm adapting. I'm just not doing it well."

"Do you love him?"

"With all my heart." In fact, said organ beat faster just at the mention. "There is no way in hell I would consent to dating a SEAL if he hadn't captured my heart and taken it with him. I'm stuck," she half-joked.

Darcy's smile broadened. "Yes. You are."

"I don't have a job. I'm mooching off my brother's fiancée at twenty-three years old. I'm lost and aimless." Her voice wobbled. A tear escaped, one of the billions of tears she knew would fall in her lifetime now that she'd made the horrifying blunder of falling in love with a SEAL. "I miss him so much," she admitted, shifting her gaze to the floor.

"I know. I know it's hard. But it won't always be this hard. There will be rough times when he's gone for months, but there will also be amazing times when he's home for even longer periods." Darcy was incredibly supportive for a woman who was in the same position as Arianna.

"I haven't heard from him in three days." This was why she was cranky this morning. Three days was an eon when he didn't call for that long. It happened. She couldn't control it. She didn't blame him. But it hurt.

Even though she'd only spent ten nights with him, her bed had felt lonely and empty ever since he left her. She often curled up in a ball and cried. For a man she'd spent ten days with. Ugh.

Arianna flinched when a knock sounded at the front door. She pushed to standing. "I'll see who it is." She hurried over to the door and opened it. And then she froze. Her breath stopped in her lungs.

Justus stood there, his smile huge, his eyes sparkling. He was in his uniform, and he looked like heaven.

For a moment, she couldn't believe it was real. She blinked and he was still there. And then she leaped into his arms.

He caught her, lifting her off the ground as he pressed her against his chest. His lips were on her neck and then trailing around to her cheek before capturing her mouth.

She slid to the ground, her feet barely touching, as he clasped her face in both hands and kissed her fully.

The door was standing open. She was certain Darcy was watching this display from behind her. She didn't care.

When he finally released her lips, she stared into his eyes. "You're here."

"I am. Did you miss me?"

"More than you'll ever understand."

"Oh, I'm pretty sure I understand perfectly." He nodded behind her. "You going to invite me in?"

She took a step backward when he released his tight hold on her. His hands were still on her waist, though. "I was just about to head to lunch with Darcy."

He shook his head. "That was a lie." He pointed behind him where Tony stood in the driveway.

Darcy was somehow already in his arms.

Arianna returned her gaze to Justus. "Wait, Darcy knew you two were coming today and no one told me?" She swatted at his chest.

"I wanted to surprise you." He smiled huge. "I missed you so much." He backed her into the apartment.

"Mmm." She wrapped her arms around him, holding him tight. "How long are you here for?"

"In theory, five days."

She swallowed back emotion. Five days. It was half the

179

total length of time she'd spent with him three months ago. It would have to suffice. She smiled. "And five nights..."

He returned the smile. "You still have that red, lacy thing?"

She giggled. "I have more than that. I've had nothing to do for the last month but wander around in the mall."

His brows shot higher. "Pack a bag."

"Where are we going?"

"My place."

"Now?"

"Yes. Unless you want me to make love to you in your brother's apartment."

She grabbed his hand and dragged him down the hallway to the guest room she'd been staying in. When they entered, she shut the door, locked it, and pushed him down on her bed. As she climbed over him, straddling his body, his hands ran up and down her butt and the small of her back.

His cock was hard. His eyes were glazed. His gaze was on her. "You really want to do this here?" he asked, smirking.

"I'm confident no one will notice or care. What do you think Tony and Darcy are probably doing? Besides, after twelve weeks of phone sex and vibrators, I need you inside me. Flesh and blood. Thick, hard flesh and blood that is nothing like any toy I own." She went to work on his belt. "This will be fast. Afterward, you can take me to your place and we can make it last longer."

He shoved her hands out of the way and released his cock by himself while she watched. "If you have an attachment to whatever panties you're wearing, I suggest you remove them now before I tear them off."

She wiggled off him, reached under her skirt to slide

the silk down her legs, and then she climbed back over him.

He grabbed her hips and held her aloft just when she would have slammed down, taking him all the way inside.

"What?" she asked, frantic need consuming her.

"I love you."

"I love you too." Warmth spread across her face.

He slid one hand around to drag a finger through her folds, spreading her arousal and using it to toy with her clit.

"Please," she begged.

"When you slide down my cock, I'm going to come in an instant. So, I'm not going to enter you until you come first." His fingers picked up the pace. She couldn't argue with that logic. Instead, she tipped her head back and let the feelings consume her. He had her on edge in moments.

She came against his fingers, her entire body jerking with the waves of pleasure. When he was apparently satisfied with her response, he eased her channel downward until he was lodged at her entrance.

"Now," he commanded.

She thrust downward, gasping at the intrusion after months of celibacy.

"Holy shit," he exclaimed, his hands everywhere.

She watched as his expression switched from awe to a tight, almost-pained look. Seconds later, he came. He kept her pinned down on his cock while the pulsing filled her.

When his breathing returned to some semblance of normal, he lifted her off him, flipped her onto her back, and hovered over her. His gaze roamed her face, her hair, her chest. "You let your hair go natural." He played with a lock of it.

"You said you liked it this way."

He met her gaze. "I'm so fucking lucky."

"I could say the same." She bit her lip. "Though to be fair, I've been a difficult person to live with lately. It's not easy. I'm lost and confused and uncertain about so many things."

"Are you uncertain about me?" he asked tentatively, his fingers coming around to stroke her cheek.

"No. Not even close. Not for a second."

"Good. We'll figure the rest out. I promise. I'm here to help."

"Now I understand why I rarely saw my relatives when they were home on leave." She squirmed next to him. "Let's get out of here before we end up staying here for five days."

Justus pushed to standing, righting his pants. He grabbed her hand and pulled her next to him. His lips landed on hers for a brief kiss. "Pack quickly. You won't need much. I intend to keep you mostly naked for the next five days."

Her heart swelled as she rushed around the room, packing a small suitcase with random things that probably made little sense. She did manage to include several nighties and even a vibrator in case they decided to get creative. After a quick trip to the bathroom, she returned with her toiletries bag. "Ready."

He took her bag from her hand and grabbed her around the waist again. His gaze was intense. "This is real for me. I wouldn't dare drag you into this world if it weren't."

She lifted onto her tiptoes and held his face. "And I wouldn't follow you if it weren't real for me."

For a moment, he simply held her, and then he rushed her out of the apartment.

It was going to be hard. The hardest thing she'd ever endure. But she could do this. She had to. She loved him.

# EPILOGUE

*One year later…*

Arianna glanced at her watch and closed her eyes. She took a deep breath and blew it back out slowly. *He'll be here*.

Except there was always the possibility he wouldn't. It happened sometimes. She'd gotten used to it. She'd learned to roll with the punches. She had a lot of friends and family who were in the same boat and had helped her adjust and adapt over the past year.

Today though… *Please, God. Just give me today*.

As she stared into the full-length mirror, she caught her mother's reflection coming toward her. She was smiling. "You look so beautiful, honey."

Arianna nodded. There was no need to ask the most important question. If Justus were in the building, her mother would have told her. "Where's Pop?"

"Waiting for me to tell him it's okay for him to come in. I wanted to make sure you were dressed."

Arianna nodded as she let her gaze wander up and

down her body in the mirror. Her dress was a simple off-white silk with lace edging that hugged her body. It was strapless because she knew how much Justus admired her neck and shoulders. Her heels were dainty with tiny stones along the straps.

She wore nothing underneath it, again because she knew Justus would find that far sexier than any bra and panty set.

Her father came up behind her. "Oh, honey, you look so amazing."

"Thanks, Pop." She smiled at him as he leaned in to kiss her forehead. "Now, all we need is a groom." She took another deep breath and held it before releasing it.

"He'll be here," her mother reassured her.

Her dad looked at his watch. "He's still got seven minutes. No problem," he teased.

Arianna closed her eyes. She hadn't seen him for a week. He'd left for a training mission somewhere outside California last Saturday. She'd spoken to him last night, though, and he'd assured her he would be there on time.

The door behind her suddenly flew open and Tony rushed in. "We're here," he said, breathing heavily while simultaneously fixing his tie.

Arianna finally breathed normally. *Thank God.*

Tony stepped in front of her and squared his shoulders. "Give him five minutes to breathe, and then we'll meet you at the altar."

She nodded. "Is he…?" She wasn't even sure what she was asking.

Tony smiled. "He's nervous like any groom, but with the added stress of knowing you were freaking out."

"I'm fine. I'm more than fine."

"*Now,*" Tony joked. "I'm sure you were in a panic until about thirty seconds ago."

"Yeah, well..."

Tony kissed her forehead and cleared his throat. "I know it's an incredible commitment, marrying a SEAL. We all know it. Justus more than anyone. I promise he loves you more than life itself, and he will do everything in his power to move mountains to get back to you for the rest of his life."

"I know," she murmured. Sometimes her brother could be more like a father, especially since he was also a SEAL. He understood.

He started to walk away, but she grabbed his hand to stop him. "This is all your fault. You're the one who hooked us up in Australia."

He rolled his eyes. "Yeah, don't remind me. What was I thinking sending my best friend off to vacation with my sister? If I had realized you had a crush on him for all those years, I would have warned him to keep his hands to himself," he teased.

She lifted onto her tiptoes and kissed his cheek. "I'm glad you're so dense. He's my everything. Thank you."

Tony smiled. "Well, I have to admit, you two are perfect for each other. I've never seen a man as crazy for a woman as Justus is for you. Except maybe myself with Darcy, of course. I love you, Sis. See you at the altar."

She was beaming as she watched him leave the room. She had the best family in the world. They might be overwhelming at times, but they were also amazing.

Justus had never been more nervous in his life. He was getting married. Until that day when Arianna had lifted her gaze to him in the lobby of that Sydney hotel, he'd never once imagined he would marry. In fact, he'd been determined to never let any woman even close enough to call her a girlfriend.

But fate had other plans. For both of them. And denying her wasn't a choice. He was madly in love with Arianna. Even though this was not a life she'd wanted for herself, she'd gone above and beyond to step up to the plate and be his everything.

She never complained. She never faltered in her convictions. From the moment she'd admitted she was in love with him, she'd changed the course of her life and been all in.

Not that life was always roses for her. He knew she cried. Sometimes she did so in his arms. He also knew she wiped those tears away and pulled it back together every time, never losing sight of the fact that she was his.

He asked the world of her, and she freely gave it to him. Every day of his life. And now, she would be his wife.

As he stood at the altar, watching the woman of his dreams walk toward him on her father's arm, he counted his blessings. His heart beat fast, and he rocked forward on the balls of his feet, anxious to have her in his arms.

She was so damn gorgeous in that dress. A princess. She deserved everything, and he would work hard to ensure she had it for as long as he lived.

As soon as Enzo passed her off to him, Justus squeezed her hand and pulled her in close, leaning down to whisper in her ear. He didn't give a damn that everyone was waiting on them to approach the altar. He needed to take her pulse. "You look so beautiful, baby. I'm sorry I was late. I love you so much."

She tipped her face up to him and smiled the smile he loved waking up to every morning she was in his bed. "I love you too," she mouthed. Her face was lit up with excitement, her eyes dancing with the love he knew she felt. Her cheeks were rosy. Her hand was shaking.

He set his forehead against hers, ignoring the chuckles coming from the audience and the fact that the minister had cleared his throat. "Will you marry me?" he asked her unnecessarily.

"Yes," she breathed. "I'd be honored."

As he led her up the steps to the altar, he breathed easier than he had in his entire life. The woman on his arm was his everything, and he was the luckiest man alive.

# AUTHOR'S NOTE

I hope you enjoyed *Hot SEAL, Australian Nights* from the SEALs in Paradise series. Here is a list of the other books in this second round:

Hot SEAL, Tijuana Nights by Cat Johnson

Hot SEAL, Hawaiian Nights by Elle James

Hot SEAL, Savannah Nights by Kris Michaels

Hot SEAL, Vegas Nights by Parker Kincade

Hot SEAL, Australian Nights by Becca Jameson

Hot SEAL, Roman Nights by Teresa Reasor

Hot SEAL, Alaskan Nights by Cynthia D'Alba

Hot SEAL, New Orleans Nights by Delilah Devlin

Please enjoy the following excerpt from Catching Zia, Book One in my Spring Training series.

# CATCHING ZIA

## SPRING TRAINING (BOOK ONE)

Chapter One

"Oh my God. That's amazing."

Zia twisted around in her seat, nearly dropping her sketch pad on the ground at the voice coming from behind her. "Wha... What?" Her heart raced as she jerked one earbud out. She'd been in her own world. The place she went when she wanted to escape and simply sketch the scenery.

Greynolds Park was the best place in the world to hone her skills.

Her gaze landed on the enormous hunk of man leaning over the back of her park bench. His face was inches from hers. But he wasn't looking at her. He was staring at her sketch.

He jerked his gaze to hers and grimaced. "I'm so sorry. Didn't mean to startle you. Or interrupt. Or...eavesdrop." He righted himself, standing tall and then pointing at her sketch pad. "But that's awesome. Are you an artist?"

Zia swallowed, trying to catch up. It was difficult. The

guy was huge. And fit. And sweaty. And out of breath. He'd obviously been running. In fact, he lifted one leg behind him and stretched it as he studied her face.

"I'm... Well, sort of." She bit her lip. Would she describe herself as an artist yet? Yes. Yes, she would. She sat up straighter and met the man's gaze.

*Why is he talking to me?*

He dropped the leg and lifted an arm over his head to stretch that elbow back. He was glistening with sweat, but it only made him sexier. His chest was rock solid and bulging with muscles. The gray T-shirt he wore was sleeveless—the sleeves having been torn off haphazardly. It was tight. Some sort of baseball logo on the front. His face was slightly red from the run, but chiseled to perfection. Strong jawline. Perfect dimples when he turned his mouth up into a smile.

"I guess you're an artist no matter how you slice it, judging from what I can see." He pointed at her sketch pad, the one slowly slipping from her lap.

She gripped it tighter to keep it from sliding to the bench alongside her. Then she lowered her feet to the ground. She'd been sitting with her heels on the bench, her pad against her knees.

His smile got brighter, and he wiped a hand on his damp T-shirt and then lifted it toward her. "Brett."

She let her gaze fall from his sun-bleached hair to his hand. He was introducing himself?

*The socially appropriate thing to do is to lift your hand and shake his and state your name.* She did just that, feeling quite proud of her ability to behave like a normal human being after the sudden disruption, and in light of the fact that he was unbelievably attractive. "Zia." She cringed when she saw her fingers were nearly black from graphite.

"I see you here sometimes." He glanced at their

surroundings and then looked back at her. "I can see why. It's gorgeous. And you obviously have plenty of material to work with."

"Uh…yeah." *He's noticed me before? Have I slipped into another dimension?* Zia was certain she wasn't the sort of person people noticed. Ever. She liked it that way.

"I hope you get paid well for those pictures." He pointed at the sketch pad again.

She scrunched up her face. "These? No. These are just sketches."

"What?" His voice rose. "You're like Picasso or something. Tell me you're kidding. I know at least a dozen people who would pay a fortune for that." He tapped the edge of the pad, careful not to smudge her work, which wasn't necessary. This was a practice pad. Nothing important.

A rush of pride raced through Zia's body. How often did someone notice or comment on her work? Granted, she hadn't put herself all the way out there yet, but she was close. "I do have some paintings in a gallery. I've sold a few. I'm hoping to have enough work soon to have my own show."

He smiled. "Awesome. I'd like to see that."

The man caused her brain to freeze. She didn't think she could possibly pull together enough sentences to continue this conversation. Should she tell him where her paintings were available? Was he really interested?

Or was he hitting on her? That thought made her mouth dry. Men didn't typically hit on her like this. Especially gorgeous specimens who looked like they owned a gym.

"If you're just getting started, do you have another day job?" he asked.

"I'm a nanny." She smiled broadly, even though she

didn't bother to mention that her charges were weeks from not needing her anymore, and she was about to become a starving artist.

"Impressive. Anyone who can work with kids is amazing. They're..." he waved a hand through the air, looking for the right words, "...confusing and...sticky."

She giggled before she could stop herself. "They're adorable small people. You just have to give them a chance."

*The sexy hot guy is still talking to me...*

"Mmm." He snapped his fingers. "Do you do murals by any chance? Like wall murals?"

"I have, on occasion. I did some for the kids I watch. And some of their friends." *You need some teddy bears on a wall in your house?* Suddenly she jerked her gaze to his left hand to see if he was married. Maybe he had kids and needed to hire someone to paint their rooms.

Nope. Or at least he didn't wear a ring. There wasn't a tan line or an indentation either, but that didn't necessarily mean anything. Some people didn't like to wear a wedding ring.

Surely he wouldn't have made a flippant statement about kids being confusing and sticky if he had his own, though.

Before he spoke again, he reached over his shoulder with one hand and tugged his scrap of T-shirt over his head.

*Holy mother of God*. He was so freakishly built. His damn chest was like a sculpture. If she had some clay, she would love to have him pose for a day and let her recreate him. Or maybe it would take two days. She might even be able to drag it out longer.

Brett wiped the sweat off his face with his wadded T-shirt. "My sister's about to have a baby," he beamed. "It's a girl. She's been looking for someone to do a mural on one wall of the nursery. Fairies or something. Could you do it?"

Ah, so there was a reason this man was speaking to her. Bingo. It wasn't because he thought she was cute or beautiful or gorgeous or sexy or whatever men needed to think to ask a woman out. It was because he needed her services.

She blew out a breath and let her shoulders fall. This was more comfortable territory than thinking he was attracted to her.

Wasn't it?

Or maybe it was actually disappointing deep down.

He stared at her quizzically.

*Shit.* He'd asked her a question. "Uh, I suppose. Yes. Does she live near here? When does she need it?"

He nodded. "Close, yes. And she still has a few weeks. How long does a mural usually take?"

"Oh, it depends. But often not more than a day or two. I can do it on my days off. Usually over a weekend."

"Cool. Do you have a card or something? I could have her call you."

This conversation was more bizarre than any she'd ever had. She didn't know this man. He could be a serial killer for all she knew. Although that wasn't likely considering how normal he seemed—if you overlooked his physique. That part was not remotely normal.

"No." She felt a flush race up her cheeks. "Haven't really needed one. But I've got a website if she wants to see some of my previous work. It's not much, but it's there." She reached into her bag and pulled out a coffee shop receipt. Flipping it over, she wrote her web address and phone number on the back side and then handed it to him.

Who in their right mind would contact her after that most unprofessional exchange? She really did need business cards if she ever expected to make a go of her art career.

Who was she kidding? An art career? She'd been slowly accumulating pieces for the last few years. But the reality was she didn't have the savings to take a risk and go all in. She needed a backup job to keep the rent paid. So, she'd been scouring the want ads for another family needing a nanny.

Maybe she was selling herself short? She sat up straighter, smiled warmly, and made a mental decision to expand her job focus. "I'd be happy to meet with your sister sometime to discuss the possibilities. If she's interested."

Brett tucked the receipt in his shorts pocket and smiled back at her. "Perfect. I'll let her know."

Chapter Two

"So let me get this straight." Monica laughed, setting her hand on her enormous belly while she did so. "You saw this girl in the park a few times, introduced yourself, and then asked her to paint my nursery?"

"Yep." He really didn't want the third degree from his sister. He still couldn't believe he'd approached Zia in the first place. Starting conversations with random women wasn't his forte.

Nope. Usually they came to him. Well, always. They had ever since he'd been about twelve and realized people considered him attractive.

But he ran the Greynolds Park path every day in the baseball off-season. He'd seen Zia sitting on that bench several times. There was something about her that caught his eye. The way her wavy brown hair was always pulled back in a loose ponytail. The way she tucked it absentmindedly behind her right ear every so often. The intensity in her expression.

The world around her ceased to exist from the moment she took out her sketchbook and pencils. She saw nothing and no one except the subject of her sketch. Admittedly, he saw her a few times before he realized what she was doing. But once he did, he knew he would find a way to use it as an opening line. He was pretty proud of that line too.

Unfortunately, he doubted Zia even heard his first statement. He hadn't factored in that she always wore a pair of earbuds and wouldn't likely hear him.

At the last second, he'd leaned closer and spoke louder than intended. And prayed she heard him.

Monica shook her head. "This seems like a bad idea. You know nothing about this woman."

"I know she's a nanny, and she's an amazing artist." He grinned widely, setting his elbows on the island in his sister's kitchen.

"Uh-huh. And she's attractive."

"Well, yeah."

Monica chuckled. "Since when do you pick up women like that? Your phone must be ringing off the hook. You've never had a shortage of people to date. You feeling like you need the challenge?"

Brett shrugged. Honestly, he had no idea what he was thinking. She was right. He almost never pursued a woman. He'd never even had a chance. And meeting someone who didn't see dollar signs and publicity first was even more difficult. If he went out with one more fake chick, he would lose his mind.

That's why he hadn't been on a date in months. Not one since the previous baseball season ended last October. And it had been a relief.

"I don't know what it is about her, but I'm drawn to her. I want to get to know her. Will you do it?"

Monica narrowed her gaze. "Does she know who you are?"

He shook his head. "I don't think so. I'd rather keep it that way." He truly didn't think Zia recognized him, and the idea was refreshing like an ocean breeze.

"Brett, I'm not going to lie for you."

"Not asking you to lie. Just don't specifically mention my profession if you can avoid it. Please?"

Monica groaned, rolling her shoulders. "What if she does a horrible job and I hate it, and you marry her and I'm stuck with her stupid mural on my wall for ten years?"

It was Brett's turn to laugh. "That's a bit of a stretch, don't you think?"

"I'm never home. I'm not even here now," she stated as she grabbed her keys from the counter and settled her purse on her shoulder. She glanced at her watch. "I need to be in the office for a meeting in fifteen minutes. How would I supervise a stranger for two days in my home?"

"I could do it." He wiggled his brows at her. "What are brothers for?"

She rolled her eyes. "How altruistic of you." Then she headed for the door. "Lock up when you leave."

"Will you call her?"

"Lord…okay. I'll call her. Tomorrow."

"Thanks, Monica."

She opened the door to step into the garage when he stopped her one more time. "Oh, and Monica?"

"Yes?"

"Please, for the love of God, don't hit on her. Let me have a stab at this one." He batted both eyes, glad she didn't have anything close to throw at him.

He could still hear her laughter after she shut the door.

He was half teasing, but only half. There had really only been one instance about four years ago when he introduced a woman he was dating to Monica and quickly found out the woman swung the other way.

Within an hour, Monica had sheepishly snatched her out of his clutches.

It had only happened one time. And of course, he realized Monica had no control over the woman's attraction to her, but he never let her forget. It was way too fun teasing her.

What Brett learned was that both he and his sister were attracted to the same type of woman. Not the flashy, gold-digger sort, but the down-to-earth, genuine sort.

He finally pushed off the island and headed for the front door. He had a website to peruse.

ALSO BY BECCA JAMESON

**Project DEEP:**

Reviving Emily

Reviving Trish

Reviving Dade

Reviving Zeke

Reviving Graham

Reviving Bianca

Reviving Olivia

**SEALs in Paradise:**

Hot SEAL, Red Wine

Hot SEAL, Australian Nights

**Dark Falls:**

Dark Nightmares

**Club Zodiac:**

Training Sasha

Obeying Rowen

Collaring Brooke

Mastering Rayne

Trusting Aaron

Claiming London

**The Art of Kink:**

Pose

Paint

Sculpt

**Arcadian Bears:**

Grizzly Mountain

Grizzly Beginning

Grizzly Secret

Grizzly Promise

Grizzly Survival

Grizzly Perfection

**Sleeper SEALs:**

Saving Zola

**Spring Training:**

Catching Zia

Catching Lily

Catching Ava

**The Underground series:**

Force

Clinch

Guard

Submit

Thrust

Torque

Saving Sofia (Kindle World)

**Wolf Masters series:**

Kara's Wolves

Lindsey's Wolves

Jessica's Wolves

Alyssa's Wolves

Tessa's Wolf

Rebecca's Wolves

Melinda's Wolves

Laurie's Wolves

Amanda's Wolves

Sharon's Wolves

**Claiming Her series:**

The Rules

The Game

The Prize

**Emergence series:**

Bound to be Taken

Bound to be Tamed

Bound to be Tested

Bound to be Tempted

**The Fight Club series:**

Come

Perv

Need

Hers

Want

Lust

**Wolf Gatherings series:**

Tarnished

Dominated

Completed

Redeemed

Abandoned

Betrayed

**Durham Wolves series:**

Rescue in the Smokies

Fire in the Smokies

Freedom in the Smokies

**Stand Alone Books:**

Blind with Love

Guarding the Truth

Out of the Smoke

Abducting His Mate

Three's a Cruise

Wolf Trinity

Frostbitten

A Princess for Cale/A Princess for Cain

# ABOUT THE AUTHOR

Becca Jameson is a USA Today best-selling author of over 80 books. She is most well-known for her Wolf Masters series and her Fight Club series. She currently lives in Atlanta, Georgia, with her husband, two grown kids, and the various pets that wander through. She is loving this journey and has dabbled in a variety of genres, including paranormal, sports romance, military, and BDSM.

A total night owl, Becca writes late at night, sequestering herself in her office with a glass of red wine and a bar of dark chocolate, her fingers flying across the keyboard as her characters weave their own stories.

During the day--which never starts before ten in the morning!--she can be found jogging, floating in the pool, or reading in her favorite hammock chair!

...*where Alphas dominate*...

Becca's Newsletter Sign-up

*Contact Becca:*
www.beccajameson.com
beccajameson4@aol.com

facebook.com/becca.jameson.18

twitter.com/beccajameson

instagram.com/becca.jameson

bookbub.com/authors/becca-jameson

goodreads.com/beccajameson

amazon.com/author/beccajameson

Made in United States
Troutdale, OR
01/22/2024

17076490R00120